PAIRED

THE ACTIVE EIGHT SERIES BOOK ONE

KRISTEN TEMPLE

Book design by JS Cover Designs
Jsdesigns93@gmail.com
www.facebook.com/jsdesignscoverart/

Editing by Affordable Manuscript Assessments
www.affordablemanuscriptassessments.com

Formatting by The Nutty Formatter
thenuttyformatter@gmail.com

ISBN: PB: 978-0-6489052-0-2
eBook: 978-0-6489052-1-9
Visit: kristentemple.com

To my son,
a love beyond comprehension.

CHAPTER ONE

I should not be here.

A lump forms in my throat as all traces of the rebellious energy that persuaded me to sneak out tonight disappear. I don't know what I expect to prove by following my cousin here. What will I say when I find her? *Hi Lily, imagine meeting you here? What d'you know, I can leave the house unsupervised and survive.* The thought of the confrontation turns my stomach because it's most likely going to end with her calling Aunt Amy. It's so unfair; we've lived under the same roof since we were three but get treated completely differently.

I remind myself that even if I get caught tonight, being grounded won't be any different to the suffocating sheltered life I already live. I pull my shoulders back, give myself a final *I can do this* pep talk, and leave the comfort of the car. The contrasting summer night air envelops me in a warm hug which helps to calm my nerves. I take a deep breath and head for the pub door.

As I step inside, a horrendous smell of vomit mixed with what I presume to be alcohol infiltrates my nostrils and it takes all my effort not to scrunch up my face in disgust. I look around the room for Lily but the only person in here is behind the bar. To be honest, his tall, staunch appearance makes him seem more like security then a bartender. He's been watching me since I entered so I figure it's now or never.

"Hi, um, I'm Kaylee, and ah, Lily works here. I think?" The words pour out quicker and clumsier than anticipated. "Do you know Lily?"

The bartender eyes me up and down and I feel as small as he makes me look. I open my mouth to say something else, but his intense gaze wipes my brain clear and I struggle to find any words.

This was a mistake.

I turn to make a quick exit, but in my moment of humiliation I neglected to notice someone else had walked into the pub and is standing right beside me.

"You said Lily invited you?" He leans against the bar and gives me an inquisitive look.

I risk a quick moment to take him in. A black leather jacket matches torn black jeans with a contrasting white shirt. His hair is short on the sides and longer but styled on top. My gaze meets his deep blue eyes and my breath catches. An invisible tug pulls from deep within my stomach and I take an involuntary step closer to him. I shake my head, trying to release the sensation.

He tilts his head slightly and I realize I haven't yet answered his question.

"Yes, I was supposed to meet her here but I'm running late." My mouth is left with a bitter taste as lying has never come naturally to me, but this guy obviously knows Lily and I'm not making any progress with the Hulk over there.

"Excuse me, Frank," the guy says, turning to the bartender, "I'll be bringing in a plus one tonight."

"You know the rules, Vincent. Invite only," Frank replies gruffly, tapping a finger on his clipboard.

Vincent's confident demeanor doesn't budge. In fact, I think he smiles even wider.

"Well consider her officially invited," Vincent responds, keeping his challenging eyes glued to Frank's.

The bartender grunts with displeasure. He gives me one last look of disapproval, then gestures for both of us to follow him. I'm so confused by what has just happened that I stay rooted to the spot.

"You coming?" Vincent asks with a wink.

I hesitate, but this could be my only chance to figure out what is going on. Before I let my mind second guess my decision, I follow Vincent around the bar and into the walk-in cooler. Instinctively, I wrap my arms around myself as the cold air washes over my body, but not a second later Vincent drapes his leather jacket over my shoulders. I shiver as his lingering body heat warms me. I lower my face into the warmth of his collar and as I inhale, I catch a hint of his cologne. It's a sweet, inviting scent which contains a subtle earthy undertone. As it wafts through me, I resist an overwhelming urge to nuzzle my face into his jacket. My face reddens from my unfamiliar reaction, and I say a silent thank you to whoever made the lighting so dim in this room.

We finally reach a door on the opposite side of the room and I'm now alone with Vincent. It dawns on me that, for all I know, there could be a secluded alley on the other side of the door. My stomach drops as my body instantly goes from desire to defensive.

"So, how do you know Lily?" My heart races, threatening to leave my chest.

"We've been working together for a while now," he responds vaguely.

"And what exactly do you do for work?" I manage to ask, despite my dry mouth.

"You'll see." Vincent smirks, then opens the door.

The noise hits me first. Music. Overwhelmingly loud music. But as my ears adjust to the blaring noise, I notice the low drum of constant chatter. The room is full of people! There's a bar lining the left wall that's obscured by the crowd, with several bar staff working meticulously to fulfill the orders. The wall behind them is covered with a multitude of different spirits, the diverse colors painting a captivating mosaic. A large cheer erupts as one of the bartenders—a tall young man—tosses a bottle into the air and catches it flawlessly behind his back.

A large section of flooring has been allocated for the dance floor in the middle of the room and it too is full of people who are dancing and drinking. On the right wall a projector screen displays an array of colorful patterns that synchronize to the beat played by the DJ.

When I finish taking in my surroundings, I step back, and Vincent places a reassuring hand on my lower back. His gentle touch awakens my body as a wave of euphoria courses through me. My mind is now acutely alert to every move he makes, to everything happening around me. He gives me a cheeky grin, as if he knows what his touch has done to me. Such confidence. No, arrogance. He leans in closer and I swear if the music weren't so loud, you'd be able to hear my heart.

"Wait here and I'll go find Lily," he shouts over the music.

When he takes a step away, I let out a long exhale.

He makes his way through the crowd, but is stopped multiple times for a handshake, hug, or high-five. The women's hands linger on him as they talk, and he wraps his arms around the shoulders of two of them and continues out of sight.

Now that I'm all alone, my nerves re-emerge. I'm not proud of sneaking out but having no freedom because of my overprotective mother, I've had to make desperate choices. Not including the handful of days that Lily has been off school due to sickness, this is the longest I've ever been on my own without Lily, Aunt Amy, or Mom. If I can prove to Lily how independent I can be, maybe she can help me convince Mom that I'm capable on my own.

I look around the room as I wait for Lily. I'm so out of place. At least Vincent's leather jacket has given my appearance a bit of an edge, but my lack of heels, makeup and body-hugging clothing makes me stand out in the worst way.

Although it wouldn't have mattered how much I'd dressed up, as I should not be here. This time it's not just because I sneaked out, but because I'm seventeen. Vincent doesn't quite look twenty-one either. Neither does anyone else here. Is this some secret underage club? It dawns on me that no one is going to care about my age and the thought releases some of the tension I'm holding in my shoulders.

My curiosity for this place drives me forward and I find myself on the edge of the dance floor. I've seen places like this in movies, but experiencing it is completely different. My senses are in overdrive, from the flashing, segmented movements of the strobe light, to the smell of the sweaty people.

I try to avoid being bumped by people moving around me, but my attempts are fruitless and lead to me being pushed further onto the dance floor. As the song changes, a beat erupts that is so deep, the pulse courses through my body. Everyone starts jumping up and down and the suffocating closeness of the people around me takes my breath away. I'm knocked about from every direction and with each bump the jacket presses against my sweaty skin. I try to push people away from me, but as I move left, I bump into a guy who spills his drink down my dress. The cold sticky substance makes a long trail down my leg and into my shoe.

My head struggles to think clearly as my eyes, ears and skin are inundated. An overwhelming pressure begins building inside me and it tightens around my lungs, making it hard to breathe. I recognize the beginnings of one of my all-too-common panic attacks. I close my eyes and try to concentrate.

I just want it to stop. Elbow into my ribs. *I just want it to stop.* Trample on my foot. *Breathe!*

The internal pressure continues to rise, pressing hard against my ribcage, begging to be released, and I concede that I can't get through the anxiety by myself. I fumble with my purse, desperate for the medication inside. My clammy hands locate the bottle but struggle to open the lid. I grip harder, willing for it to yield, and my whole body relaxes when it finally listens.

"Kaylee–" A voice calls out behind me and I turn to the familiar voice. A sense of calm begins to filter over me as I take in Lily, but then a large guy barges into my side, sending the medication flying out of the bottle as I fall to my knees. A sharp intense pain radiates through my legs.

I bite back against the pain as I scramble my hands along the floor to locate a pill, but my hands only make contact with the sticky residue from spilled drinks. *No!* I stare down at the dance floor wide-eyed, gasping for air as a sense of hopeless-ness washes over me. The overwhelming pressure that had been building intensifies and it has a grasp on my body so fierce that it aches against my skin, begging to be released. I close my eyes and let out an involuntary scream as I push firmly against the ground. As if unlocking a door, the pressure violently pours out of my body, leaving a sense of weightlessness in its wake. A cold chill lingers in the air, sending a shiver through me, and my arms shake as they struggle to find the energy to keep me from collapsing.

My weary eyes open and as I take in the wide empty circle of space surrounding me my breath catches. Those closest to me stare at me wide-eyed while they hold onto each other to regain their balance. I can only imagine that in their haste to get away from 'the freak', they fell into each other.

I slowly rise to my feet, not knowing how to respond. As I glance up there's a clear line to the bar and to Vincent. He's looking at me with the same fearful look as everyone around me. Vincent presses his hand up against the bar and a sudden rumble underfoot causes me to lose my balance. Everyone around me grabs on tighter to the person beside them while ducking to the ground.

Wait.

Earthquake?

A piercing scream echoes through the club and I'm knocked about as people move in unison toward the exit. My heart races as I attempt to push my way through the crowd, the panic rising again, but a familiar presence helps to calm me as Lily links her arm around mine.

"Come with me, my car is out the back." She doesn't look at me, but I can tell she's furious.

"I've got Aunt Amy's car," I inform her.

She nods, then releases me. Elbows jab at each other as we all cram through the walk-in cooler and outside the pub. I continue running until I reach the car. Once I'm inside, I tug too quickly on the seat belt which sets off the safety catch. Again and again I pull, but it refuses to extend beyond those few short inches. I let out a frustrated groan but command my hands to remain calm and gently glide the seat belt down until it clicks in place beside my waist. My heart is racing, and my lungs are burning as though I've run a marathon. *Just breathe, Kaylee.*

I know I need to get moving. If that was an earthquake, the last place I want to be is stuck in traffic. The car jolts forward as I try to take off too quickly, almost causing it to stall. I recollect myself and finally get away.

I should not have come.

As I speed home, my mind races back to the club and I try to make sense of what happened. I don't think I'll ever forget everyone's eyes staring at me in horror. Were they scrambling away from me or had there been an earthquake while I was having my panic attack and I just didn't feel it? North Carolina has been known to have the odd earthquake every year or so, but it's something I've never experienced before and hope I never have to again. The panic as people tried to hurry out was chaotic.

And the nerve of Lily! She was supposed to be working but she's been out clubbing.

I'm so embarrassed about my panic attack. I've always had my medication with me so have never had an attack that strong before. And that was supposed to be my chance to prove to Lily that I'm fine being on my own! What will she say to Aunt Amy? And no doubt they'll tell Mom. Mom might even be furious enough that she comes home from work to deal with me.

A thought quickly crosses my mind not to go home. I imagine a version of my life where I get to live by my own rules, doing whatever I want, whenever I want. I begin to smile but quickly wash it away as I grudgingly accept the dependency I have on my family. I'm still in high school. I've never had a job and have no money. Hell, I've never been on my own for more than a day.

As I pull into our driveway, I can't see Lily's car so I must have beaten her home. Even better, the house lights are still off. I quickly turn the car off and make my way to the back door as silently as possible. *Please let Aunt Amy be asleep!*

I don't know who's watching over me tonight, but Aunt Amy isn't awake. As quietly as possible, I place her car keys back in the key bowl then slip into my room and let out a massive sigh of relief. As I undress, I realize I'm still wearing Vincent's jacket. Now, in the privacy of my own room, I unashamedly nuzzle into the collar of his jacket and take in his sweet earthy scent. The smell is so enticing, and courses through my whole body. My mind wanders to the moment he leaned in closer and I imagine those soft lips pressing against mine. Heat radiates across my face, but I quickly shake my head and press my palms into my cheeks to try and cool down. I groan at the fact I'm embarrassed just thinking about a kiss. Never being allowed out on my own and constantly moving around has made relationships basically impossible. I take off Vincent's jacket and hide it in the back of my closet, along with any other thoughts about him. There's no point even thinking about it.

A noise outside captures my attention. Lily's home. I turn off my bedside light and quickly climb into bed. Lily's footsteps move softly down the hallway and I hear her stop outside my bedroom door. I hold my breath as I wait for her to come inside, but she never does. The soft click of her door announces that she's gone to bed. I guess it's a discussion for another day.

CHAPTER TWO

My blaring alarm wakes me from a deep sleep, and I groan as I reach over and turn it off. Last night I spent over an hour tossing and turning, trying to still my mind, and then I kept waking every couple of hours, anxious about today's confrontation.

Clatter downstairs tells me that someone is awake, but I'm hoping Lily has given me the decency of talking to me before telling Aunt Amy. I slowly get ready for school, trying to hold off the inevitable, but with time running out I have no choice but to get this over and done with.

Lily sits quietly at the kitchen table–fortunately alone–with coffee in hand. Long gone is the precise dramatic makeup and curve hugging black dress of last night. And her long curly brown hair is now up and tidy in a bun. Does Aunt Amy know what her daughter gets up to when she's supposed to be working?

I sit across from Lily and try to present my case before she has a chance to chastise me. "I know what you're going to say, and you're right, what I did last night was wrong and I'm sorry, and I promise if you don't tell Aunt Amy, I won't do it again."

"What you did last night was stupid and reckless, Kaylee, and because of you we were almost exposed," Lily replies more firmly than I expected.

"That's a bit harsh. It was the earthquake that had people running out and exposing your little club." I raise my hands to air quote when I say *exposing*. "You're just mad I found out that you're partying, not working."

I know I've taken the childish response by trying to turn the tables on her, but sneaking out isn't as bad as her lying about going out partying instead of working, so maybe I'm the one holding all the cards?

Her phone buzzes on the table and she huffs as she quickly presses *decline*. She opens her mouth to speak but slowly closes it, seeming to choose her next words carefully. "I think we should talk about what happened last night."

I groan. Of course, she wants to talk about the anxiety attack. "I had a panic attack and my outburst scared a few people. Sorry! Can we just pretend last night didn't happen?" As much as I might be holding the cards, I really don't want Mom finding out. I might be here under Aunt Amy's roof but I'm most definitely under my mother's rules. I can tell she's struggling with the decision, so I try a different tactic and deflect. "On the other hand, you should introduce me to Vincent."

She raises her eyebrows. "Not in a million years. Vincent isn't good news."

I must admit, I had asked half-jokingly, but her response makes me feel more deflated than it should. What did he do for her not to like him? And how well does she know him? She's never spoken about him before.

Lily is only two months older than me but has always

acted like a much older sister. She's protective and stern, but we haven't been close in years.

Lily's phone rings again, breaking me from my dazing, and she lets out a grunt of frustration and presses *decline*. "We'd better go, or we'll be late for school, but this conversation isn't over."

───────

THE SCHOOL DAY DRAGS ALONG PAINFULLY SLOWLY, especially because of exam blocks. The stupid rule that dictates students can't leave until the exam time has finished means I'm left sitting at my table with nothing to do for the next half an hour.

As I look around the classroom, I know that no one here will miss me when we move over the summer break. By now I've come to accept the lack of meaningful friendships as part of the package when you practically start a new school each year. With Mom being deployed most of the year I'm stuck with Aunt Amy and Lily. Completely opposite to my mother, Aunt Amy is a whimsical, lovable sort of person. The only downfall is that we're constantly relocating because of her job. She's a primary school teacher but will only take maternity leave positions. Her words ring in my mind, *Life is too short to be tied down to one place.* It also means that I've never felt what it's like to belong to a place or a group of people. I always hear friends raving excitedly about their weekends together, with their secret handshakes and matching accessories. I play it off as if I couldn't care less, but deep down I wish I had the opportunity to experience that.

I cannot wait until I'm old enough to leave home. I've learned by now not to think about it. I've wasted so much energy rebelling against moving and my strict upbringing that it ends up making me emotionally exhausted, which stirs my anxiety. Unfortunately, a life of moving around so often means I've grown to be an introvert, and last night's panic attack is evidence of what happens when I'm out of my comfort zone.

I slump deeper into my seat. My anxiety attacks have never caused that sort of reaction before. My face begins to flush from embarrassment. For my own sanity I try to convince myself again that they were stumbling because of an earthquake I somehow didn't manage to feel.

And I know Vincent saw my panic attack. He was staring right at me when I stood up. I don't know why I care about what he thinks. I don't even know him, and it's not as if I'll ever see him again. After last night's episode, if we do cross paths, he won't want anything to do with me. The thought makes my head hang in sadness.

Oh, get a grip, Kaylee!

I jump in my seat as the teacher announces that there is one minute left of exam time, and my cheeks flush as I glance around the classroom, unreasonably thinking everyone has just heard all my inner thoughts.

With the exam finished, I catch up to Lily to head home.

"Only one more week to go," I say with enthusiasm.

"Let's hope the next school is a bit more exciting."

I groan. With only one more year of school left, I hope that the new school will be the last I ever have to go to.

Lily's phone rings again, breaking me from my thoughts. She presses her thumb repeatedly against the *decline* button and I stare at her, waiting for an explanation.

She shakes her head at me as if to say *don't ask.*

She should be grateful. My mom has always been strict about technology whereas Lily was allowed a phone when she started 'working'. Maybe she can persuade Aunt Amy to let me 'work' with her? I figure now is the best time to try and plead my case.

"Here me out."

Lily rolls her eyes but remains silent.

"In a few short months I'm going to be in senior year, and then who knows after that. But all I know is that I can't stay cooped up at home all the time. Please, please, please help me persuade Aunt Amy to let me go out with you, or to even get a proper job? Something, anything, to get me out of the house!"

She gives me the usual frustrated look that I get every time I ask. "I've tried, Kaylee, I really have. But your mom is the one who needs convincing, not Mom or me. You need to remember that your mom does this because she thinks it's the best way that she can protect you because she's not here to do it herself."

I swear she has that speech on standby because I've heard it a million times. I may have panicked last night, but I want that chaos, the sensory overload, and the freedom. While I had felt suffocated in the middle of the dance floor, it was nothing compared to the feeling of being trapped in my own life.

I know I'm acting like a child, but I stomp away from her, irritated that the one person I can talk to can't even pretend to be sympathetic. Unfortunately, I can't go far as she's my ride home.

As I reach the parking lot, I can't contain my excitement. A pickup has parked behind Lily's car, blocking us in, and leaning up against it is the stylish blue-eyed boy from last night. His form-fitting jeans and shirt don't leave much to the imagination, and the schoolgirl inside me giggles with appreciation. *Play it cool, Kaylee.*

He dips his glasses down when he sees me coming and gives me a cheeky smile. "Well you've been a hard person to track down."

He's been looking for me?

I try to keep calm as I keep the conversation lighthearted. "Are you sure I shouldn't turn around and run? It seems I've found myself a stalker."

Lily's finally caught up and she is furious. A raised finger points straight in Vincent's direction. "I told you last night to stay away from her."

He raises his eyebrows at her. "Maybe if you'd answered my calls, I wouldn't be here."

Lily turns to me. "Please, just get in the car and wait for me."

She's begging me but telling me to stay away just makes me more intrigued. I know I'll never get this chance again, so I stare right into Lily's eyes and firmly say, "I'm going to go with Vincent. He's offered me a ride." I lie about the last bit but hope he's willing to oblige.

She glances frustratedly between the two of us, and Vincent gives her a *what can you do?* shrug.

She looks me straight in the eyes with nostrils flared. "If you take one step toward him, I'm calling your mom."

My breath hitches. Lily isn't messing around. I look at Vincent and deep inside that tug pulls again toward him but this time I allow myself to continue walking.

"Kaylee..." Her voice trails off, obviously taking the hint that she can't stop me if threatening to call Mom didn't work. She turns to Vincent instead. "Vincent, please. Don't."

Don't what?

He doesn't reply to Lily, just looks at me and says, "Let's go," with a wink, and I swallow back any hesitation and get in his pickup.

———

"I DIDN'T REALIZE YOU WERE LILY'S PAIR WHEN I MET YOU last night." Vincent breaks the silence lingering between us.

"Do you mean my cousin?" I ask, confused.

"If you say so." He chuckles as he shakes his head.

I stare at him, wondering what he's trying to insinuate but he doesn't elaborate.

He's driving in the opposite direction to where I live so I ask, "Where are we going?"

I haven't been allowed to venture out of Asheville much which is frustrating as North Carolina has so much to offer.

"It's a surprise," he says with a grin. "It's a little bit of a drive, but I'll bring you home later this afternoon if that's okay?"

For the first time I'm being offered options. It's amazing how freeing it feels. I smile and confirm that it's fine.

We drive south-west of Asheville and I give Vincent a questioning look as we start driving into the forest. I clear my throat as that unease from last night returns from when we were alone in the cooler.

And this is the exact reason I tried to convince my mother I needed a phone. Alone with a stranger in the woods, with no way to contact my family. What could go wrong? I shuffle in my seat.

Vincent seems to notice my hesitation and laughs. "I'm not a serial killer."

"I'm sure every serial killer says that before they strike," I joke, but my heart still races faster than normal.

"If Lily thought I was at all capable of hurting you, she would have set this pickup alight before letting you anywhere near me. Wouldn't she?"

I wouldn't go to that extent but yes. Lily would have done

anything in her power to stop me if there was something sinister about Vincent. The thought puts me at ease.

"I want to help. I saw what happened last night." As his words come out my head hangs in shame. I was hoping he wouldn't bring this up.

"Just let me show you something. Any sign of hesitation and I'll take you straight back to Lily. Promise." He places his hand over his heart.

I'm not sure why I trust his words, but I agree.

The pickup starts to slow down on a long stretch of road, and I wonder what's wrong. He turns to the right and the vehicle bounces around as he drives off the road. I brace against the door frame as we make our way down a barely visible dirt track. I'm being shaken around so much that I have to clench my jaw shut or risk my teeth clashing together.

About a mile in, the ground smooths out and he continues along the dirt track. Strange that the dirt track starts smoothing out here and not at the road. I go to ask Vincent a question but something in the distance captures my attention. I can barely make it out through the trees, but I'm certain at the end of the road I spot a cabin.

CHAPTER THREE

As we make our way closer, we break through the rows of pine trees into a small grass clearing, at the back of which is a beautiful cabin made from wood of a rich auburn color. At the front of the cabin is a small open balcony, almost willing me to come closer and relax upon it. The hours I could spend there looking out into the wilderness or staring up into a starry night...

"Do you live here?" I ask, curiously.

He chuckles. "No, my grandfather does. The old man hardly leaves so I just restock the pantry." He signals to the backseat which is covered in bags of groceries. I smile. Long gone is the cocky guy from last night, replaced with someone caring and considerate.

"Meeting the family already?" My face blushes as the words escape me, meant to be a joke to myself.

He smirks but doesn't say anything more.

He parks his pickup under a wooden carport and grabs out the groceries.

"I'll be back in a second."

While he's gone, I look around. I stare out at the open

clearing in front of the cabin. A small dirt path breaks off on my left and leads to a stream. The water is so clear that even from here I can see the rocks at the bottom. I take a deep breath in and let the fresh air flow through my body.

Vincent re-emerges from the cabin and moves toward the clearing in front of us. "Coming?"

I follow him to the center of the clearing, and he sits down on the grass. He doesn't begin talking until I join him on the ground.

"I want to tell you a story." He smiles at me eagerly.

I nod as I smile back, intrigued at where this is going.

"Everything on Earth is at a certain point within the cycle of life and death, starting and ending with the energy source that most call Mother Nature. For example, a seed uses Mother Nature's energy to grow into a plant, but eventually it will die, decompose, and become nourishment for the next plant. It's the same for an animal that has grown through consuming her nutrients. When it dies its body also decomposes and provides energy back to her."

"Okaaay…" I have no idea where he's going with this conversation.

"Many, many years ago there were people who could harness Mother Nature's energy and achieve incredible feats such as creating life, manipulating the weather, and seeing the future..." He looks me in the eyes. "They were called witches."

A small chuckle escapes. Seriously? Witches?

He rolls his eyes at my reaction but continues talking. "Unfortunately, people couldn't see that the witches' main purpose was helping to establish balance within nature, and eventually they were all hunted and killed.

"While people today can't harness energy the way the witches did, by surrounding themselves in Mother Nature's bounty," he gestures around us, "and attempting to become one with her, they can temporarily open themselves up to receiving a little of her energy. This meditative practice gives them a short burst of clarity and vitality."

I feel as if this is a joke and Vincent is about to turn around and start laughing at me for being entranced in his talk of witches and meditation, but he doesn't.

"Why are you telling me this story?"

"As I said, I want to help after what happened last night."

I don't know whether it's pride or humiliation, but his statement gets on my nerves. What makes him think he's qualified to help with my anxiety? That look I gave him after the panic attack must have triggered something in him as he's certainly trying to be my knight in shining armor, coming to the rescue.

I take a quick moment to mull over his words. He wants me to try meditating for my anxiety? I once had a therapist who had recommended meditating, but it didn't make a difference, although I won't tell Vincent that. He seems quite sure of himself and a little knock back to reality won't hurt.

For now, I'm just happy to be in a position—for the second day in a row—where I get to make my own decisions and feel I'm not being chaperoned. "Well let's get on with it then," I say, hoping to be over with this part of the afternoon sooner than later.

"Perfect. Take off your shoes, get comfortable and close your eyes."

I follow his commands, relishing the soft grass under my feet before I position myself cross-legged.

"I'm going to guide you through an exercise, and I want you to really concentrate on what I ask you to do. Try and block out any thoughts that come into your mind that pull you from the task. Okay?"

Yep, he sounds exactly like my old therapist!

I nod in reply. I can tell he's serious about this meditation business, so I'll try my best to do what he requests.

"Great. First off, I want you to focus on what you can hear."

With my eyes shut, my senses are already heightened. I try and target my hearing and the most abundant sound is the birds chirping in the distance. I vocalize that.

"Good. Now listen deeper."

I stretch out my hearing and listen to the rustle of the leaves and branches swaying in the wind. Again, I convey that to Vincent.

The answer seems to satisfy him, so he continues with his demands. "Now turn your attention to what you can smell."

The first word to come to mind is *fresh*. It smells so clean and untainted by us humans, which makes my heart ache at the state of our major cities.

I notice my thoughts have strayed and I follow Vincent's original request to redirect them back to the task at hand. *Concentrate, Kaylee. What do you smell?* It's so hard to pinpoint what makes up the smells around me. It's fresh and sweet. The grass, the flowers, the flowing stream. All I want to do is take in a deep breath and let the purity course through my body.

I don't reply verbally but the next command comes after giving me adequate time to contemplate and delve deeper into my answer.

"What can you feel?"

I turn my attention to my whole body and a gentle wind blows on my face and the warmth of the sun radiates on my skin. The grass underneath me is soft and cold.

All my senses are becoming heightened and all-encompassing.

"Now, without opening your eyes, I want you to visualize everything that you're sensing. Try and see where each item belongs."

Having just walked out onto the opening, the scene is still fresh in my mind. I can visualize the stream and the trees, the clearing.

"Don't just focus on the larger items," he commands, as if reading my thoughts. "Everything is made up of a collection of smaller pieces. See the trees as a combination of the rough, strong bark and their twisted branches. See each grain of dirt and growth of grass. See each droplet of water."

I focus on one item, to really visualize it in my mind. I recall a yellow flower that was beside my leg and try to break it down. I consider how many petals it might have, the number of leaves, the roughness and contour of the stem and the roots growing down into the dirt. It catches me off-guard how absorbed I am in this task. *Maybe Vincent might know a thing or two?*

I hadn't recognized that my mind had wandered, but Vincent's voice brings my attention back to the task. "Try to feel yourself connected as one to these items, Kaylee. As if there are invisible cords between you and everything around you."

I can hear his enthusiasm grow and it makes me concentrate harder.

Feel myself connected through invisible cords? I place my hands on the ground and pretend there are thousands of tiny threads extending from my hands and that they connect to everything around me in the image I've concocted in my mind.

"Now, imagine that each item you're connected to is full of Mother Nature's energy, and that you have access to this life source. See that energy, imagine connecting to the energy, and harness it."

When I think of energy, the sun comes straight to mind with its golden bright light. I focus on the items my imaginary threads are attached to and visualize each item filled with a golden hue.

As I create this image, the threads seem to vibrate, hungry for that golden light. I give in to the sensation and imagine each thread is a straw, allowing it to drain the golden essence from the items and transferring it into my body.

As I move through the motions, a small moan escapes my lips as if I've bitten into the most delicious dessert I've ever tasted. It's as if my body is being fulfilled by this imaginary energy, like a warm, wholehearted hug from the person you love the most. Slowly, my body becomes lighter, but more complete.

I'm startled as a warmth overlays my hands. With his hands on mine he whispers in my ear, "Let me help you."

My hands tingle, the same way as last night, as an intense sensation flows through me. My body awakens again, empowered and strong. My eyes burst open and Vincent is right in front of me, beaming with pride. I'm elated and, for the first time in my life utterly free.

When our eyes connect, my breath catches as an overwhelming desire to wrap my arms around him courses through my body. I don't know how to react as I've never experienced these feelings before, so I quickly look away while pulling my hands out from under his.

"This is amazing!" I say, trying to deflect. I feel so weightless I'd swear I'm not touching the grass, and quickly check just in case. This didn't happen when I meditated with my therapist! I guess I owe him an apology, even though I didn't verbalize my disbelief. "How is meditation not a bigger thing if people around the world are experiencing this?"

He rubs the back of his neck, his voice soft. "Normal people don't experience this."

"But you said that people meditate to experience this feeling?" I reply, confused.

"Yes, and people try to do that. But what they experience isn't even a fraction of what you're feeling right now. Normal people aren't capable of getting more than just a little bit of a high."

"Vincent, what's going on? Are you trying to say that I'm some sort of freak?" His constant replies telling me that I'm not normal are making me confused and hurt. My defenses continue to build, and I'm inundated with thought after thought that there's something wrong with me, that I'm broken, that I'm useless. It's as if the heightened energy inside me has magnified my emotions, and right now I'm stuck on the negative ones. I can't seem to make it stop and an all-knowing sensation of panic begins to rise. I grab at my heart as a strangling sensation wraps around my chest, and gasp as my lungs struggle to fill with air.

Vincent's trying to talk to me, but my ears fill with a high-pitched ringing as I fight to breathe. He places his hands on my cheeks and stares deeply into my eyes. "It's okay!"

My body goes limp, too weak to even sit up. Vincent gently lowers me back on the grass and I stare at him wide-eyed, trying to figure out what has just happened.

"You're not a freak." He says the words slowly with emphasis. "And if you are then I am too, so you're not alone." He has the audacity to laugh.

I slowly make my way into a sitting position, my mind hazy. "What did you just do to me?" My breathing is ragged.

"The exercise I just guided you through is what we call

regenerating. Our bodies have the ability to harness external energy, and every time we regenerate, we're basically fueling our body with additional energy from Mother Nature. What I did was take away that energy from you." He gives me a cheeky smile.

"Well that explains why I'm so exhausted." I nudge him with my elbow.

I ponder his statement for a moment. I–well technically he keeps saying we–can make ourselves feel energized? I've never heard of such a thing before. And what is the purpose of it? I ask Vincent that very question.

"Remember earlier when I said that witches would harness Mother Nature's energy to fuel their gifts? Well, the same thing applies to us."

He pauses for a second then places his hand on the ground. I watch him intently, too uncertain to move and not yet fully comprehending the meaning of his words. Suddenly stems sprout from the ground and bloom the same yellow flowers I saw earlier. My face distorts as I'm overwhelmed by their abundantly fruity smell. Not that it's a horrible smell, but it's as if my body recognizes it shouldn't be there.

My mind scrambles to put together the pieces.

I look up at Vincent in shock. Okay, I'm no longer playing games.

"What was that? How did you do that?" I struggle to find one single question to get a logical explanation for what just happened. "What are you?"

He smiles as his eyes find mine. "What are *we*."

CHAPTER FOUR

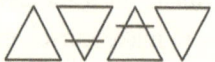

A loud alarm erupts from Vincent's pocket, causing me to jump in fright. Vincent pulls out his cell phone and swears when he sees the time.

"I've got to get to work but we can continue the conversation on the way to your place?"

I almost let out an audible groan. Whatever this is, what we are, I need to know more.

Once we're back in his vehicle, I have a chance to mull over what has just occurred and everything Vincent has said. He's saying we're not normal. That we have... powers. "So, are you trying to say that we are witches?"

"Not quite. Think of us more as carriers."

"Carriers?" I repeat, confused.

"Our powers stem from a witch who could control the four elements: earth, air, water and fire. The witch was about to be captured and instead of letting her powers cease to exist, she transferred them to four humans, each to carry the gift to control one of the elements. We are part of the youngest generation who descend from those four humans. I can control earth. Given your wind outburst last night it's not hard to see where you come from. As I said earlier, I'm here to help you with that. It's the least I can do for causing all this mess."

My head is swirling with information and a nauseous feeling courses through me. I wind down the window to let in fresh air and the cool wind blows over my face. I take a deep breath and it helps to settle my stomach.

Had I not just seen it with my own eyes I would have thought Vincent was crazy. He said I had a wind outburst last night. My mind crosses to the moment I looked up to the empty space around me, and everyone stumbling for balance. I take a sharp inhale. That was my power? So, Vincent saying he wanted to help had nothing to do with my anxiety. He had seen what happened last night and knew what I'd done.

My mind replays his last words.

"How could you possibly think you're responsible for my outburst?" I ask incredulously.

He shifts in his seat. "When people come to my club, I share my regenerated energy with them without them knowing. It helps to keep the party alive. I didn't realize who you were so when you came into the club, I'd passed some energy to you."

That tingling sensation I'd felt under his hand! I had felt it again in the clearing when he put his hand over mine and a rush of energy entered me.

"When we start using our gifts, we begin with learning to regenerate, and then it can take weeks to learn how to use it to fuel your element. When you started panicking though, you somehow tapped into your gift and used that energy I shared to create the wind attack." Silence lingers between us. "I'm sorry." He turns to me briefly, his eyes filled with honest regret.

My mind doesn't know where to start with all the information I've gathered this afternoon. I try to sift through it all, but each revelation makes me want to ask three more questions. His apology irks me though. I can't even begin to wrap my head around everything, but why does he think he needs to apologize for it? Lily's last words ring clear in my head *Vincent, please. Don't.*

Don't what? Don't spill the secret!

I turn to Vincent ever so slowly. "Lily knows about me." It's not a question but a statement.

He doesn't say anything, just stares ahead at the road. The road that's leading me back to home.

A deep rage begins building in my stomach. Lily knows. And she's never said anything. Even begged Vincent not to tell me. Does Aunt Amy know too? And Mom?

My breathing hitches.

He'd said we were part of the youngest generation, which means this would have been passed on from one of my parents. I never knew my father. Mom always said that they hadn't planned on having children so soon in the relationship and he left after he found out she was pregnant. Was it from him? Or Mom? Either way she must know! Is this why my life has always been so sheltered? Am I so much of an abomination to her that I can't be trusted on my own? My stomach knots in pain and I squeeze my eyes shut, trying to hold back the tears.

Vincent remains silent, leaving me to sort through my thoughts. I choose my next words very carefully and speak slowly. "Vincent, I've known you for two days and in that time, you have been more honest than anyone I have ever known. Please don't take me home. I'll sleep on a couch, or even the floor, but I just want answers and you're the only person I can trust to be straight with me."

"Look, I–"

"Please," I beg, cutting him off before he has a chance to decline.

He lets out a small laugh. "If you'd let me talk, you'd hear me try to say that I'm about to head to work, but why don't you come along, and we can discuss it later? Maybe some time to work through it all might make you feel better? I'll be busy most of the night, but that'll give you time to think."

It's not a no. I'll take that for now.

"What is it you do for work?" I try diverting the conversation. Right now, I don't want to think any more about what I've just found out. The tension in my stomach is still twisting in knots at the lies my family have told me my whole life.

He rubs the back of his neck. "If I had to label it, I'd say I'm a party planner. There's an eighteenth birthday I'm helping with tonight."

"Are you sure it's okay for me to be there?"

"It'll be fine. Just..." he hesitates, "let me do the talking."

————

THE PICKUP BEGINS TO SLOW DOWN SO I PRESUME WE ARE close to the destination. We must be just on the outskirts of Asheville. Vincent pulls into a long driveway and an immaculate two-story house comes into view. Clean white walls encase large glass windows, with precisely trimmed hedges surrounding the house. He parks close to the house, beeps the horn, then gestures me to follow him out. He begins to untie the load in the back of his pickup, and I gasp as multiple kegs are unveiled from underneath the covers.

What have I got myself into?

Vincent shrugs in response to my gawking. "Kids will always find ways to access alcohol. At least this way I can help to keep it regulated."

I'm not sure what to think, but before I get a chance to say anything a group of teenage boys emerge from the house and greet Vincent. One of the boys is strangely familiar but I can't quite place him.

"Sam, Kaylee. Kaylee, Sam." Vincent introduces us. "He's my bartender for all these gigs."

That's where I remember him from, he was working at the club last night. The bartender with the fancy tricks.

I give him a handshake and a friendly smile which he reciprocates.

A blonde cheerleader type girl bounces out from behind the guys and wraps her arms around Vincent. She stares at me as she plants a kiss on his cheek, and I avert my eyes. It seems to be the response she was after as she lets him go and smiles.

"And this is Brittany, the birthday girl," Vincent informs me.

"Kaylee," I respond as cheerfully as I can pretend.

Vincent leans in and whispers something to her and her shoulders soften.

She turns to me and rolls her eyes. "Girl, let's get you ready for tonight." She links arms with me, and before I know what's happening, I'm being led away.

Brittany takes me inside and leads me upstairs to what I presume is her room. It's the largest bedroom I've ever set foot in. A large canopy bed sits in the center with white flowing drapes falling to the floor. Behind her bed is a large glass window that has a view of the afternoon sun setting behind the forest. She opens the doors to her closet–which is close to the size of my bedroom–and tosses me a pair of shorts and a singlet.

I look down at my over-sized shirt and jeans. Apparently, it's not good enough for her. "Thanks." I try to sound grateful but it's hard when she's obviously being judgmental.

"Anything for Vincent's cousin. You're so lucky to be related to him. You have to tell me everything about him." She accentuates *everything* and stares at me eagerly.

Her comment throws me off-guard. Cousins? Is that what he told her earlier? He had said to let him do the talking.

"Ah... distant cousins who never really see each other. So, I don't really have anything to tell you." What is with all the lying lately?

"Damn. Oh well, I'll just have to keep using my good old southern charm." She flicks her hair over her shoulder and leaves me to dress.

I hold up the shorts and my stomach drops. They are the shortest shorts I've ever seen and once they're on I double check they cover what they're supposed to. Her clothes cling to me in ways mine never have, but when I look in the mirror, I'm pleasantly surprised. The shorts seem to accentuate my legs, which I'm more than happy about as I tend to be on the shorter side of average. And the singlet does well to flatter my curves, which have only developed in the last year.

I pull my long brunette hair out of the ponytail, wrangle it into a messy bun and take a moment staring at my reflection. Something in the mirror seems off and I wonder if it's the different clothes, but then I finally realize I'm smiling. A true heartfelt smile. Despite my lingering rage toward my family, I can't help feeling excited for what's unfolding. I've grown up feeling like such an outcast to my peers. But Vincent is saying I'm part of a *we.*

I'm surprised my brain isn't scrambling for some sort of explanation for what has occurred. It's as if his words have resonated with me, and something deep inside knows it's the truth. Has Lily told Aunt Amy or Mom what's happening yet?

She threatened to call Mom. Well, if that's the case, I better make the most of tonight.

I make my way downstairs and look out over the room in surprise. In that short space of time the party size has already tripled. Vincent's across the room talking to a group of people, shaking hands and high fiving the way he did last night. Is it in those moments he shares his energy? To *keep the party alive* in his words. He looks up and when he sees me, he stops talking and stares. He says something to the group then makes his way over with his cheeky smile.

"You seem to be settling in well." He motions to my attire.

"Yeah, I think Brittany wanted to make sure she was taking good care of your cousin," I reply sarcastically, rolling my eyes.

He rubs his neck. "Sorry about that. But it worked didn't it? I'll be busy most of the night keeping an eye on everyone, but I'll try and check to see how you're going when I can. Do you think you'll be all right? Otherwise I can organize another ride for you to get home."

"No!" I reply louder than anticipated. Right now, that still isn't an option for me. "I mean, no, I'll be fine."

He chuckles. "Okay, well come and find me if that changes."

Once he's left, I'm not too sure what to do with myself.

I glance around the living room. The chairs have been pushed against the walls and a DJ is setting up in one corner. Just off the living room is another area with a pool table and a ping pong table. The gaming area, I suppose.

The kegs have already been set up in the kitchen, using the island as a bar counter. Sam grabs a cup and attempts to pour the first drink and it sputters a heap of foam. He doesn't seem concerned as he keeps pouring, and eventually the golden liquid appears. The crowd around him cheers and they line up to get the festivities started.

The energy in the room is contagious and I find myself excited for the afternoon.

I hadn't consciously joined the line-up, but I end up at the island across from Sam. He pours me a drink and I stare at it on the bench.

"Thanks, but I don't drink."

He gazes at me, puzzled, then chuckles. "Well you seem to be in the wrong place for someone who doesn't drink."

I take in the guy before me. He's a tall, stocky guy with kind eyes and jet-black hair. He gives me a warm smile and it helps to settle my nerves.

"It's not so much that I don't drink, it's just that I've never drunk before." The heat rises on my neck as I spill my truth but he's genuine enough not to laugh.

"Look, I'm going to be behind the counter all night. If you want to drink, I'm happy to keep an eye on you, and if it looks as if you've had enough, I'll cut you off."

By now my cup has already been grabbed by another person, so he pours another and puts it in front of me. After everything this afternoon, my mind can use some extra help to stop over-thinking. I hesitate a second longer, grab the drink, and down it before I have a chance to change my mind.

I try not to cough as the warm bitter taste flows down my throat. How do people enjoy this? And often!

Sam tries to hide his chuckle, for which I'm thankful.

He continues to serve people around me, but I don't have anywhere else to go so I keep close by. Every time I think about leaving to find someone else to talk to my stomach ties in knots. Sam hasn't told me to get lost yet so I don't think he's too bothered.

"So how did you end up working with Vincent?" I'm

basically shouting now as the music has been turned up as the place fills with people.

"I moved here three months ago and was searching for a job. I ended up at a party he was covering, and his bartender didn't turn up, so I offered to step in. He only has these parties at the end of every term but because of the risk I'm taking with this chosen career choice, I get a higher income and don't have to work in between."

"You mean the risk in illegally supplying underage people with alcohol?" It comes out sounding more judgmental than I expected but he doesn't seem to flinch. Something about this situation hasn't sat right with me since I discovered what was in the back of Vincent's pickup.

"Whether we are here tonight or not, these kids would have found some way to access alcohol. What Vincent and I do is provide an environment where it's safer for them to do so. I'm on the bar the whole night monitoring how much everyone is drinking, and Vincent roams around to keep an eye on everyone. If either of us feels someone is over the limit, then we speak to the host to let them know their friend is cut off. If anyone is caught supplying them with anything for the rest of the night, then Vincent and I pack up the alcohol and leave."

Whatever way he tries to justify it, it still doesn't change the fact it's illegal. I stare at the newly poured cup of beer that Sam's given me and figure I should decide on whether I can accept it or not. It'd be hypocritical of me to dislike what they're doing but still participate. I've been trying to prove I'm capable of making my own decisions so why should anyone else here be denied that same option? Most of the people here will be in college next year, and in some countries would already be of legal age to drink. It's also nice to think the teenagers have Vincent and Sam keeping an eye on them.

I take a sip of my drink. I think it's going to take some time to wrap my head around Vincent's involvement of supplying alcohol to minors, but I'm on board with everyone having their own choice of whether they participate.

"How do you know Vincent?" He's now shouting so I can hear him over the music.

I have to think about an appropriate answer. For some reason when I think of the truth–that I only met him last night–it seems reckless of me to be here with him.

"He's friends with my cousin," I reply. "You might know her. Lily. She was at the club last night."

His interest piques. "Yeah, I've seen her there a couple of times."

He tries to say something else, but I have to ask him to repeat himself two more times and I still don't understand. I point to my ear and shake my head to indicate I can't hear him. I hadn't realized how busy the house had become. There's no longer a clear pathway to move around. I look into the living room and catch Vincent talking with Brittany. She throws her head back in laughter and runs her hand along his arm. He reciprocates with his perfect smile which causes a wave of nausea to run through my stomach. I've seen this act before at school, when the girl puts on an over-exaggerated performance to try and entrance the guy, but this time it feels different. I should turn away, but my body doesn't move.

I mean, I don't blame Vincent for his interest in her. She's the envy of every girl in this room. Everything about her screams perfection and she knows it.

I down the rest of my drink as she runs her hand through his hair. I imagine the feel of his soft hair gliding through her fingers as she reaches around the back of his head. My stomach pangs again and I tear my eyes away before the inevitable unfolds.

Fortunately, Sam's too busy serving people to notice my entrancement. I hold out my cup to him in hopes of cutting the line and he rewards me with another cup of liquid gold. I give him a smile and motion that I'm going to leave, and he gives me a look of encouragement.

I turn around and take two steps before I'm face-to-face with Lily.

CHAPTER FIVE

Lily grabs me by the arm and drags me through the crowd and outside, away from the blaring music.

She looks at me sternly. "You have two seconds to come with me and go home. You can thank me later for covering with Mom. She thinks you're with a study group at school studying for exams next week."

A laugh escapes me. "You're delusional if you think I'm going anywhere with you." I look her directly in the eyes. "I know everything."

Her fists clench at her sides as she looks into the house. "I'm going to kill him. How dare he–"

"Him?" My voice rises and I'm practically yelling. I've never spoken to her like this before. Maybe it's because of her lies, or the alcohol, or a combination of both. "How dare you!" I'm furious. I press my palms firmly against the side of my body to stop my hands from shaking. Her first response isn't to try and deny anything, or even to try and explain. She's annoyed the secret is out!

"Me? You have no idea what we have all sacrificed to give you this normal life," she screams back.

"I never asked you to do that! I was never given a choice on what I wanted. No one has ever cared about what I wanted. But I'll save you having to worry about me anymore because I'm not going back home anytime soon. All that's left there is lies and deception." My chest heaves up and down.

Her mouth gapes. "You're such a selfish brat. You've got nowhere to go so get in the car before I call your mom."

The threat doesn't even make me flinch. I'm more than ready to have this conversation with Mom.

"She'll be staying with me."

I turn to the voice behind me and Vincent is leaning against the door frame with arms crossed.

Lily turns to him, rage plastered on her face. "You had no right!" she says with a finger pointed at him.

"After last night's episode there's nothing you can say to me about having no right." He talks calmly despite Lily's anger.

"You want to meddle in our business? Fine! She's all yours then. Good luck dealing with Maria."

"She knows where to find me," he says with a shrug.

He knows my mom?

Before I get a chance to think further on it, Lily storms off.

"Did you forget you're working?" Vincent calls after her but the only response is a middle finger raised in the air toward him which makes him smirk.

So that's how Lily knows Vincent. She works for him at these illegal parties. I guess she technically wasn't lying when she said she was working last night. I doubt Aunt Amy knows where she's working, though.

I turn back to Vincent. My head is starting to spin from the effects of the alcohol, and I decide that right now that feeling is a lot better than the anger, the hurt, the confusion of everything I've learned. I turn back inside toward more alcohol. Vincent follows closely but doesn't say a word, seeming to understand that right now I'm done talking.

As I make my way around the house, I'm intrigued by the sounds coming from the gaming area. The ping pong table is surrounded, and I squeeze through the crowd to get closer to the table. There are cups on both ends arranged in a triangle, and people take it in turns to bounce a ping pong ball at the cups at the opposite end to where they're standing. One finally lands in a cup and everyone cheers. A girl at the end where the ball lands stares at the cup, a look of disgust on her face. She reaches down to pull the ball out and then throws her head back, downing the contents in the cup.

I'm completely captivated in the game. There are five people in each team, rotating after each throw and it's not long before one side has had their cups emptied. The call for the next five players to challenge the winning team goes out and I take a deep breath as I step closer to the table. The winning team members walk around the table through the volunteers to choose their next opponents. I lock eyes with the least intimidating member and give her a nice smile. This game is exactly what I need! She smiles back and motions for me to take a spot at the table.

My excitement is short lived. Five bottles of liquor are placed on the table, and each cup is filled with small portions from each bottle. I assess the amount in each cup and figure it's about two large mouthfuls. I swallow hard at the thought of downing one of those drinks.

One of the team members holds out a bag to me, instructing me to grab out a ball which will have a number to identify my playing position. I dip my hand in the bag, moving my fingers over several marble sized balls and make a quick decision on which to grab. I pull a ball out and turn it around until the number is displayed. Number one.

My hands are already clammy by the time I take my place at the end of the table and I look up to find the girl who picked me is first up too. Being the winning team, they get to throw first, and I wait in anticipation as she lines up her shot. She releases the ball and it bounces on the table then lands straight into a cup. The crowd cheers at my misfortune.

My stomach drops. I shake my hands as I pep myself up for what's about to come, then reach down to collect my prize. The smell hits me first and sends a stinging sensation down the back of my nostrils. There's no way I'm going to be able to drink this with my sense of smell intact. I pinch my nose then chug the drink.

I was wrong. It's three large mouthfuls of alcohol. I take in an audible breath and stabilize myself on the table. My chest feels as if it's on fire. I stare at the girl and she smiles mischievously. Least intimidating my ass!

Someone passes me the ball and it takes a moment to register what to do—my body is still recovering from the recent assault. I carefully gauge where I need to aim the ball to ensure it only bounces once—as per the rules—and wait with excited anticipation as the ball moves over the table. It hits the rim on one of the cups then ricochets off the table. The girl gives me a smirk and we both make room for the next two players.

Each team has ten cups in total, and by the end of the fifth round, nine have been drunk on each side—two of which I've consumed. The girl and I take our positions and a wave of nausea courses through my stomach as I imagine having to take another drink. She releases the ball, but it is thrown too far to the left. I let out a sigh of relief.

I line up my next shot, but purposely make sure my aim is

off. As much as I want this game to be over, I don't want it to be by winning as that would mean I'd advance into the next game. I don't think my body can handle another drink. I make a fake disappointed face as the ball misses the target, and make a silent prayer that the next shot goes in.

My prayer isn't answered. Shot after shot the ball misses the cup, and before I can understand what's happening, I'm taking my place at the table again.

The girl moves her arm back and forth to practice, then finally releases the ball. A lump forms in the back of my throat as the ball moves with precision over the table, then bounces into the last remaining cup.

I swear a small bit of bile just rose in my throat.

I stare at the stupid white ball floating in the brown liquid and try to hold myself together as my stomach attempts to empty its contents. Everyone in the room starts chanting, "Chug! Chug! Chug!" and I have no option but to lift the liquid to my lips and take those three long dreaded mouthfuls.

I can't do all three in quick succession, so I take a breath in between each mouthful, but slowly and surely, I finish the cup and throw it down on the table in defeat. The opposing team cheers at winning another round which seems unfathomable. These people have more pride than sense.

As I step back from the table, everything has already started to slow around me. The music overwhelms my hearing, making it too difficult to have any sort of conversation so I make my way closer to the DJ and join the crowd that fills the living room. I walk on unsteady legs, and tell myself not to drink any more.

Everyone sways to the music and I squeeze into the middle of the crowd to join them. As each minute passes, the alcohol takes a stronger hold and I lose myself deeper, letting all thoughts of today wash out of me. My body moves with no restrictions and I don't care how it looks, just that it makes me feel freer than I have ever felt in my life. The sweat clings to my skin as one song follows another and the available space around me gets smaller and smaller. Instead of the claustrophobia I felt last night, I welcome the closeness tonight.

The movement in the room seems to shift as people's inhibitions relax to the effects of the alcohol. Eventually they've all turned to each other to dance, their hips moving against one another.

A guy to my left moves closer and gives me a smile, swaying in front of me as an invitation to dance. I step back, happy in my own little bubble, but he doesn't get the hint and grabs my arm, pulling me into him. I can smell the alcohol on his breath, and I try to push him away, but he reaches around my back and pulls me in closer.

I'm caught off balance as his hands are pried from my body. Vincent pushes the guy away, to which he throws his hands up in surrender and leaves.

Vincent looks at me with his enchanting eyes, creases of worry crossing his forehead. "Are you okay?" he shouts over the music.

"Where's Brittany?" It's the first time I've tried to speak since I've played the game and it comes out jumbled, which makes him smile, but he's still able to understand me.

He leans in closer to talk and my heart flutters. "Trying to find someone who's actually interested."

He motions to the other side of the room where Brittany spins around, dancing back and forth between two guys. I can tell they both want her attention, but it appears they're getting fed up with the competition. Neither seems like the type to back down though.

I turn back to Vincent and my drunken body allows my

walls to drop and does something I'd never dream of doing sober. I reach up and run my hand through his hair. The front is rough from the gel he uses to style his hair, but as my hand passes to the back of his head my fingers run through his smooth–and surprisingly warm–hair. I let out an embarrassed chuckle as I drop my hand by my side and stare at his perplexed face.

He goes to say something, but we're interrupted by commotion on the other side of the room. The two guys Brittany has been flirting between are wrestling each other, attempting to throw punches whenever a hand is free. People quickly join in to try break them up–friends I'm presuming–but they too get caught up in the fighting and start shouting profanities back and forth which eventually leads to throwing fists too.

"Crap," Vincent shouts. He looks toward the kitchen, I presume to find Sam, but he can't be seen, and the commotion is growing larger. He pulls a whistle out of his shirt and starts blowing on it, but it can hardly be heard over the music.

He grabs me by the arm and attempts to pull me through the crowd but the people in front of us act as a barricade.

"Fight! Fight! Fight!" the shouting grows louder as those around the commotion stupidly move closer and chant to the group of boys fighting each other.

Two of the boys wrestling are thrown into the crowd, knocking those around them to the ground. They scramble to get up, but one girl remains on the floor. I catch a glimpse of her, and she isn't moving. The girls are screaming at the boys to stop and a handful of people who try to break up the fight end up getting hit in the process.

The helplessness I felt last night begins to resurface, tightening around my lungs. My palms sweat as my body tenses. The situation has escalated so quickly. I grab my purse but quickly remember I lost all my pills last night when they scattered across the dance floor.

We can't afford a repeat of last night.

I tug on Vincent's arm and the panic must be clear on my face as he swears when he looks at me. He stops trying to get us through the crowd and presses my back against a wall.

Vincent quickly double checks over his shoulders. He places his palms on the wall either side of me, encasing me between him and the wall. His forehead furrows with concentration and his arms tense beside me. The floor begins to rumble as it did last night and déjà vu strikes again as everyone screams in panic, reaching their arms out to each other for balance as they shrink closer to the ground. The earthquake lasts only a second but it's long enough for the music to be cut off, and in the short space of silence when everyone inhales from screaming, Vincent stands on the armrest of a couch beside us and blows his whistle again. This time the whistle carries over the crowd and everyone halts to attention.

"Everyone get out!" Vincent shouts.

No one moves. The shock over the proceedings in the last minute roots everyone to the spot.

He blows his whistle again. "Now!" he yells furiously to the crowd, pointing to the door.

He seems to be the oldest person here, even if it is only by a year or so, but they all seem to understand the extent of what just happened with the earthquake and the fight and start making their way outside.

The adrenaline within me starts to subside but my head is still spinning from the effects of the alcohol. I'm more hindrance than help, so I sit on a couch and wait.

Sam is over by the girl who had fallen and assists her to her feet. Fortunately, she doesn't look hurt. Vincent is sternly talking to Brittany and the two guys who initiated the fight. They all hang their heads. My eyelids heavily blink a few times and I allow them to close for a quick second.

My eyes open as Vincent lifts me into his arms. How long have I slept? I try to look up at him but the room spins, sending a wave of nausea through my body.

I attempt to say, "Not home." It comes out mumbled, but he gives me a small nod.

I press my head into the warmth of his chest, and close my eyes, praying that when they open again everything will finally be still.

CHAPTER SIX

I wake with a forceful jolt. As I open my eyes, the blinding light causes a sharp pounding in my head and I cover my face with the sheets to try and shield myself from the assault. A familiar scent infiltrates my body but this time there's less of the sweet cologne smell, and more of the earthy undertones. It takes a second to connect the scent with my location and my heart races.

I slowly lower the sheet as my eyes adjust to the morning sun and gently run my hands along the top of the covers. I lie still for a minute longer and try to put the pieces together.

The room is encased with timber walls and flooring. I must be back at the cabin. I remember falling asleep at the party but recall nothing about getting into the vehicle or here. I search for a clock or phone to see what time it is, but his room is filled only with the essentials. The only sentimental item seems to be a photo frame on the side table picturing two older women. Vincent's eyes stare back at me from one of the women and I smile at the picture of his mother.

Was she the one to pass on his gift?

I don't even know where that thought came from, but it

makes all the information from yesterday flood back into my mind. My head is still foggy because of last night's alcohol, so it struggles to hold onto any information. Maybe it was all a dream anyway? My stomach knots as I fail to convince myself otherwise.

I take a moment to go over everything that happened yesterday. Somehow a meditative practice can fill me with an abundance of energy and that energy can be used to control air.

I let out a cackle, the sort that says I've gone insane.

There must be a different explanation for what he did with those flowers. But what? I decide I can no longer wait for answers and head out to try and find Vincent.

I almost fall over as I get out of bed, my legs not willing to cooperate. Headache. Foggy mind. Lack of bodily control. This must be what a hangover feels like. There's a glass and some Tylenol on the side table and I figure it's a wise decision to take all the help I can get to shake off how horrible I'm feeling.

I slowly make my way to the living room and there's a sudden calming change in the atmosphere. In the middle of the living room is a beautifully carved timber coffee table, surrounded by a wooden couch that is covered in simple cushions. The couch faces a rock wall that has a fireplace built into it. It must have been lit recently as the smell of burned wood lingers among the fresh air. There's an exquisitely carved wooden dining table and chairs off to the right, and behind that is the kitchen.

There are minimal decorations, but the attention to detail in the items within the room makes the place come to life. I realize that what I'm feeling is a sense of home. The longest I've stayed in one place is sixteen months, so I've never really felt at home anywhere. I embrace the sensation, which puts me completely at ease.

The cabin is empty, but a noise from outside draws my attention. I step out onto the balcony and shield my eyes from the sun directly above me which is causing the sharp pain in my head to re-emerge.

As my eyes adjust, I spot Vincent in the center of the clearing, his back turned to me. His shirt is off, and as he moves, his muscles strain across his tanned back.

Three large earth mounds stand on the farthest edge of the clearing, a good quarter mile away. The mounds are perfectly shaped into rectangles, like a target. Vincent's hands are raised to shoulder height, but nothing is happening. Suddenly a thick, long branch comes flying toward him from the clearing and stops just out of reach of his hands. He never takes his eyes off the three targets but continues to move his hands in a flowing pattern as the branch in front of him separates into three pieces with the front of each thinning down to a point.

With a quick, thrusting motion of his arm, the three pieces of wood fly forward and hit each target in the center with a loud thud that causes me to jump. I lift my hand to my mouth in shock.

Vincent turns back around toward the cabin and pauses when he notices me. The three barriers and the protruding wooden pieces sink into the ground as if nothing was ever there.

As he reaches the top of the balcony, he wipes himself down with a towel and puts his shirt back on. It still clings to his body, conforming to his muscular physique. He shouldn't have even bothered with it.

"Tell me everything." It's all I can manage to say.

"Good morning, Kaylee," he says with a smile as he takes

a seat beside me. He runs the towel over his hair, causing it to spike up. "It'll make more sense if I give you a bit more information about our history."

I nod my head, ready for the truth.

"In the early 1600s there was a witch named Charlotte who could control the four elements. She wholeheartedly believed her powers had a purpose to keep the peace on Earth and the only thing she feared about being captured was the ending of that power. One day she made the ultimate sacrifice and exposed her abilities to extinguish a fire that was blazing through the community school. A handful of parents offered to hide her for her selfless gift, but instead she saw the good within their hearts and asked only one thing–to pass on her power to them.

"She knew no ordinary human would be able to contain all her power, so she asked for four women, each to carry the ability to control one of the elements. She explained that she would perform a ritual, and once finished they had to procreate, and her power would infuse with their unborn children. What the volunteers didn't know was that to pass on her gifts, Charlotte had to relinquish her life source too. As the last drop of her essence left her body, she collapsed lifeless to the floor.

"But true to their word, each woman procreated and bore a child that was gifted an element. This gift has been passed along through the generations, and we are part of the youngest generation."

He pauses and waits for his words to sink in. Had I not seen it with my own eyes I don't think I would have stuck around as long as I have. Witches and powers? And somewhere along the lines I fit into this.

How could my whole family keep this from me? What exactly is it that they think I can't handle? Or are they just trying to hide the fact that I'm not normal? I know at some point I'm going to return home, and who knows how they'll respond. Will they try to keep me from this information? From Vincent?

I look up at him, desperate to learn as much as I can. "So where do we go from here?"

Vincent smiles. "Now the training begins."

He stands up and motions for me to follow him to the center of the clearing.

"Yesterday I guided you through some steps to try and regenerate. Learning to regenerate is essential to everything that we do because it is the energy that fuels your element. The energy we gain from regenerating is the same that is provided to all people through eating Mother Nature's boun-ties, but we can bypass the consuming food component, and access much higher quantities."

Bypass eating? "So, if I never wanted to eat again, I could just regenerate all the time?" I ask, shocked.

"You could, by why would you want to? Imagine a life without pizza, or chocolate." He shakes his head as if the thought is too unimaginable. "There are risks with regener-ating that you need to understand. Once you learn how to harness the regenerated energy, you can then give it to and take it from other people."

I recall yesterday when he withdrew all my energy and I couldn't even hold myself upright.

"But you need to be careful." His voice has turned stern. Serious. "As you have felt already, regeneration makes you extremely contented and the effects last a lot longer than eating. And receiving energy from someone else, as when I shared to you, fulfills you even more than regeneration alone. However, stealing it from someone is most satisfying of all." He gazes off as he mentions stealing. "Unfortunately, stealing energy has its consequences and it wouldn't be good if dead bodies started showing up around the place." He chuckles and rubs the back of his neck.

The color drains from my face. This could kill people. "Have you killed anyone?" I wait nervously for his answer.

"No," he quickly reassures me, but he won't make direct eye contact. "Although I know people who have. Stealing can become highly addictive and it can get to the point that you can't stop yourself and end up completely draining a person's life source."

My hands fidget in my lap as we sit together in the middle of the clearing. For the first time I'm getting a sense of the danger from these abilities.

Vincent looks at my restless hands and pulls something out of his pocket. "You don't need to worry about hurting anyone."

My mouth gapes as I stare at the taser in his hands.

"Just a precaution," he says with a nervous laugh. "Shall we get on with regenerating?" he casually adds on.

It takes a moment to move past the fact he's holding a weapon to subdue me if the need arises. I look up at Vincent and I get a sense of angst, concerned that I'm not going to be the person he seems to think I am.

I close my eyes to try and block out the outside world, because otherwise I know I won't be able to focus, especially with that taser in his hand. I think back to yesterday and how he guided me through regenerating by opening my senses. I try and follow those previous instructions and open my hearing, explore my sense of touch, and visualize where I am. When I'm finally calm and centered, I imagine that golden light beaming in everything around me. Instinctively I want to reach out and grab it, and I let my inhibitions go. I scrunch my hands into the grass and inhale deeply as I imagine that energy flowing through thousands of threads and into my body.

Knowing what to expect this time, I welcome it. That magnificent, overwhelming sense of fullness and stamina. I keep my eyes shut and focus my full attention on the energy to prevent it from overwhelming me as it did yesterday. It buzzes through my body, ready to escape at any chance. I grab a hold of the wild beast inside me and attempt to slow it down. Then I speed it up. Then I direct it to my stomach, my legs, my hands. I make any possible attempt to gain some control.

An idea pops into my head and with my eyes still shut, I reach out my hand with palm up. I'm hoping Vincent understands what I'm asking for, as talking right now would interrupt my concentration. A couple more seconds pass then he places his rough hand gently on mine and I cover it with my opposite hand.

I direct my energy to my hands and sense the weight of it pressing up hard against my skin, like an imaginary door, and know I need to concentrate, otherwise it will all spill out once that door is opened. When I believe I have enough control I carefully open the channel. The energy holds strong on my side of the door and I let out a long breath as I ever so slowly release that golden force.

Steady, steady. I repeat to myself.

It inches slowly across the threshold from me to him, and when I've passed on enough, I attempt to stop the flow. My forehead strains as I try to pull the energy back enough to close the channel, but it resists against my hold. My grasp on the energy slips as the pressure becomes too much and it floods out of my hands into Vincent.

My energy slams up against a wall. I open my eyes and Vincent is a few steps away from me. He must have recognized what was happening and let go of my hands. *Thank God he didn't use the taser on me!* I lie back on the grass panting, exhausted from passing on too much energy, and I welcome the warm evening sun against my skin as I calm down. The pressure in my hands subsides as the energy disperses throughout my body. I'm expecting Vincent to be mad at my failure, but he's beaming.

"Not bad Kaylee, not bad at all," he teases.

I look at him, confused. "But I lost control."

"No, you did great," he reassures me. "At this pace we'll be on to element training in no time."

I smile and let myself relish in the fact that maybe I can do this.

"You ended up passing on quite a bit of energy so it will probably be a while before you have the stamina to regenerate again. If you get to the point that you deplete your supply, then rest is the only thing that will help you recover. For now, I'll give you a little bit back. When I do though, I need you to focus on accepting that power and not taking it, do you understand?" He stresses the last sentence.

I nod my head and he helps me to my feet, keeping his hold on my hand.

I focus on his hand underneath mine and sense a warming sensation run between them. I imagine that his incoming energy is a deep blue color, a replication of his eyes, and visualize the blue threads coming through into my hand and twining around my golden energy to create a beautiful masterpiece.

The weight of the energy inside me is heavier than when I regenerate solely, but I get a sense that I'm not completely full. The deep blue energy stops flowing, and I experience a strong urge to grab hold of it, knowing there's more on the other side that I could take. My grasp tightens in his and

Vincent gives me a warning, "Do not steal it," but doesn't remove his hand from mine.

A guttural growl begins in my chest, and the sound shocks me enough to come back to reality. I open my eyes and apologize for my outburst.

"It takes a lot of restraint not to steal. You did really well," he says gently. "How do you feel?"

The abundance of energy courses through my body, and I delight in the vitality. "I feel amazing," I reply with a smile, letting go of my previous transgressions.

His hand shifts in mine and my stomach knots, realizing that we haven't let go of each other. It's now well past the point of subtly removing it. *Do I slowly let go? Quickly let go? Pretend I need my hand to move some hair off my face, so he doesn't think I'm rejecting him? Am I rejecting him? Do I keep it there but risk him rejecting me?* My heart races as I figure out what to do.

His thumb gently brushes against the back of my hand and as I wonder if it was intentional, a movement from behind Vincent startles me and I quickly drop his hand. A robust gentleman, with a bow and quiver strapped over his shoulder, moves toward us. He raises his hand and waves. I must admit I'd stereotyped his grandfather as a typical elderly person, but as this extremely fit man comes into view, I stare in astonishment. He's just as in shape as Vincent. His face gives away his age, though. He has a tidy gray beard covering his jaw, with tired blue eyes that look as though they've seen sights I don't even want to imagine.

"You're the splitting image of Maria," he announces, coming over with arms wide open to embrace me.

Strong arms wrap around me, his warmth heating my skin.

"You know who my mother is?" I ask, confused.

"Of course, your mother and my daughter were paired for eighteen years." He smiles kindly at me, then shifts his gaze, a tremble pulling at the corner of his mouth.

The word *paired* resonates with me and I recall Vincent using it yesterday when he was talking about Lily and me. I'm not sure where Vincent grew up but perhaps it's something to do with friendship or family? I make a mental note to ask Vincent later as now doesn't seem like the right time. Vincent's demeanor seems to have saddened, too.

"Come inside, my child, it seems we have a lot to catch up on." Vincent's grandfather speaks to me with a kind tone, and I find myself being drawn to this gentleman. I've only met my grandmother once, so I've never really known what it's like to have grandparents.

Once we're inside, I figure now is the right time to ask him if I can stay.

"I hope you don't mind Mr..." I trail off, not certain what his–or Vincent's for that matter–last name is.

"Please, just call me Pop," he answers, picking up on my unspoken question.

I repeat the name a few times in my head to get accustomed to it, but I find that it feels fitting for him.

"I hope you don't mind, Pop, but I'm going through some family problems and Vincent's the only person I felt I could turn to. I just needed to get away for a night or two." Saying it out loud has finally cemented the fact that I really don't have any idea what's going on anymore, and the only people who might help are sitting in this room. My eyes sting as I fight back the tears.

"Your mother was always such a free spirit as a child," he replies, completely off track. "She hated being contained and was always begging to be outside. God forbid if you told her no." He releases a deep chuckle. "She was so gentle and kind and loved everything wholeheartedly." He pauses as if in reminiscence.

I listen intently as he describes someone completely different to the regimented, strict mother I know.

"It was heartbreaking to watch that little girl be squashed down deep inside as she became accustomed to our way of life. She was so resentful, and to be honest I didn't think she was ever going to consider having a child, knowing what was going to be passed on. Having you, though, seemed to restore that passion for life inside of her. She was so determined to try and give you the life she never had.

"Sophia—my daughter—told me how Maria planned to keep this life hidden from you and I honestly thought she was delusional. But all Maria wanted was time to try and make this world a safe place for you, and the rest of us."

It's as if he's trying to spin me the same story that I've heard all my life. That everything my mother is doing is for my own good. I think he's expecting me to be grateful or understanding but it only makes me angry. If this is all true, then my whole life has been a lie.

I furiously pick at my nails as I delve deeper into my thoughts, forgetting that I'm halfway through a conversation with Pop. I'm so angry and upset. Based on what I've been told, both Mom and Lily know what I am, which means Aunt Amy must as well. And it's not just what I am, it's what Mom is as well. When a tear runs down my cheek, I quickly wipe it away and shake my head, trying to clear my thoughts.

Pop stands up, bringing me back to reality, and places a warm, reassuring hand over mine.

"You're welcome to stay here as long as you need." He gives me a kind smile and heads off to the kitchen.

I turn to Vincent with glazed eyes. "It's all true, isn't it?"

He nods, even though I already know the answer.

"Thank you for telling me," I say as sincerely as possible.

"As I said yesterday, you didn't give me much of a choice. Plus, I am partly to blame for all this."

"Well, I'm glad it happened. Thank you again."

He gives me a heartfelt smile and I reciprocate it.

The afternoon passes by, filled with small talk between Pop, Vincent and me. Something about this place makes me feel I've known these two my whole life.

"I best be heading home," Vincent finally announces. "I should be back tomorrow, but if I'm not here, take the time to practice regenerating. It's the foundation for everything that we're able to do."

I nod in understanding, and we say goodbye.

Once he's gone, I find myself desperate for a shower. I look down at my–well Brittany's– clothes and groan. I've run out of clean clothes. By now it's too late to head back to Asheville, and my stomach ties in knots at the thought of having to go back tomorrow to pack a bag.

I scan the room and find myself wandering closer to Vincent's dresser. My hand pauses on the handle. *Surely, he won't mind?*

I slide open the drawer and run my hand along his neatly folded clothes. I pull out a shirt and some shorts and make a mental note to make sure I change out of them before he arrives in the morning.

After a quick cold wash down, I try his clothes on. Not surprisingly, the shorts are too big, but the shirt is long enough to cover me to mid-thigh, so I forget about wearing shorts. I make a quick dash back to Vincent's room for the night and settle into his bed.

I shake my head. Today has been... incredible. Eye opening. More than I could ever dream. But at the same time filled with so much anger and pain. This morning I was trying to find some logical explanation to explain what was happening, but now I don't even question it. From the beginning I've felt a connection to Vincent. Is it because we share this power? When I look back at how I went with him after school without even knowing him, and am now staying in his room without question, there's something inside me that knows I can trust him.

I ponder how long I will stay here. I can imagine time is running out before Aunt Amy or Mom tries to drag me home but there's no way I'm letting them keep me away from this life. No matter what they try to do, I know that this power is within me and no one can stop me from harnessing it.

I curl up tighter under the covers and my body readily welcomes sleep after such a mentally exhausting day.

CHAPTER SEVEN

My eyes blink heavily, but I finally accept that I need to wake for the day.

The cabin is empty, so I take Vincent's advice and get straight to training. When I step outside, the sun is directly overhead again. I'm going to lose so much training opportunity if I keep sleeping in until lunch!

I quickly move to the clearing in front of the house and focus on what I want to achieve today. I've seen Vincent regenerate without having to close his eyes, so I decide to try and regenerate faster and more efficiently.

I take three deep breaths to ground myself, then look around and take in everything around me that I'm going to use to harness energy: the grass, the trees, the flowers. The options are limitless. Despite having my eyes open, I still try to envisage that golden hue encompassing everything I see. Once I achieve that image, I open my body to be one big vessel, ready to take in the energy. I create imaginary channels between my feet and the items around me, and visualize that golden hue emptying from nature, moving through the ground in my imaginary channels then into me via my feet.

Like yesterday, the invigorating feeling of being completely energized rushes through me and I smile. I open my arms wide, and lift my face to the sun, taking in a final deep fulfilling breath. *I hope it always feels this amazing.*

The sound of a car approaching distracts me and Vincent drives into view. He exits the pickup and walks toward me with a familiar backpack.

"Figured you could do with a change of clothes." His eyes run over me from head to toe and I blush as I consider how bad I look. And probably smell. This will be the third day wearing these shorts and shirt. But at the same time, I'm extremely grateful. He's saved me having to face Lily and Aunt Amy.

After a quick outfit change, Vincent offers a suggestion. "Using your gift doesn't just take mental strength but also physical. There's another place we can train a short hike from here which adds in some exercise if you're keen?"

The idea of exercise makes me groan but I nod in agreement.

He follows the dirt path beside the cabin which leads to the stream, and we begin an uphill journey. With silence between us, I become entranced with my surroundings. The wind blows through the trees, rustling the leaves complimented by the sound of water flowing lightly downstream. Small mammals scurry away as we walk past, and birds chirp a beautiful melody in the background. I don't think I've ever been this absorbed in nature before.

"How long is this walk?" I ask after a couple minutes, my lungs and thighs already burning.

"About half an hour uphill."

I groan again and Vincent lets out a chuckle.

"I want to try more than regenerating." I need to learn as

much as I can, as quickly as possible from him, on the off-chance Mom or Aunt Amy tries to drag me away.

"Okay, but only if you can regenerate in the next thirty seconds." He stares at his watch.

My heart races at his challenge, but I'm ready for the task. I continue from my training earlier today but have to concentrate harder as my feet move across the earth, allowing energy to enter for split seconds only as each foot touches the ground. I draw it in quickly, alternating between feet, reveling in the sensation as it expands through my body. I hold it, feel its weight, and take control. I look at Vincent and smile.

"Fourteen seconds. Not bad." He gives me an approving nod.

"What's next then?" I ask with determination.

"The next step is connecting to your element. It's exhausting work so in the beginning you will use all your regenerated energy just to grab a hold of air. As you continue to train, it'll take less and less effort and eventually you'll be able to achieve bigger and stronger maneuvers without much effort at all."

My excitement builds. What will I be able to accomplish? "So, how do I connect with my element?"

"There's a connection between you and air, similar to the link you create when you regenerate. You need to make the connection, then figure out how to send commands through with arm movements." He raises his arms and some rocks on the ground lift into the air. With a thrusting motion the rocks fly forward following the trajectory of his arms. "Connecting to the element is usually the easy part. Figuring out the code for communication may take a few days or even weeks."

My excitement wavers. *A few weeks?*

"Unfortunately, there's no one-size-fits-all approach to

using to your element. I was young when I first started and even though I could connect to earth within a few hours, it took a couple of days before I could send through commands." Vincent reinforces that I need to be patient. "There's a lot you can do with your element, so I found it easier to focus on one task at a time."

"What did you do first?" I ask, searching for inspiration.

"I crafted my own puppy out of dirt. I was never allowed a pet when I was younger." As he talks, rocks and dirt around us collects and forms a puppy in front of me. It runs around in circles chasing its tail, and then disintegrates. I initially smile but then recall all the times I begged Mom for my own pet but couldn't have one because we moved around so much. My heart aches for that little boy who just wanted a pet too.

I can tell we're getting close to our destination as our pace begins to slow. As we continue, the sound of running water grows louder. Vincent finally stops and when he looks at me his eyes are beaming.

"Close your eyes."

How can I reject such a happy face? I oblige and allow myself to be pushed and pulled the last few steps, trusting in my companion.

"Okay. Open your eyes," he instructs.

I'm awestruck by the sheer beauty of my surroundings. The hill flattens out, making it seem we've reached the top when in fact we haven't. A large grassy field makes up the center of the clearing, with trees that continue around to the left and right and cease when they hit a rock wall across the far end of the field. Water cascades over the top of the rocks, creating a majestic waterfall which collects into a pool at the base. The water is clear blue, matching the bright sky, complimenting the multiple arrays of green surrounding us in the trees, grass, and moss. Over the top of the rock wall, the forest continues uphill.

"Where are we?" I ask, amazed.

"I'm not sure. I came across this place a few months ago, and I've never seen anyone else here."

"It's beautiful!" I'm so captivated, I can't manage to say anything else. He waits patiently while I take in my surroundings.

"I think for this part it would be nice for you to have time to yourself. If you need me, I'll be by the water."

He leaves me alone in the middle of the opening.

So first I need to figure out how to connect to air, but what then? When I think of air, all that comes to mind is wind, so maybe just grabbing control of the wind?

Vincent said that creating a connection to air would be similar to regeneration. He guided me through an exercise of opening my senses to nature, so perhaps I can open my senses to air? I close my eyes and as I breathe in and out, I let the freshness of the air expand through my lungs, opening myself to the smells carried in the air. Next, I turn to my sense of touch. It's a humid day and the air hangs heavily. Suddenly, a gust of wind comes by, blowing my hair behind me. It's a cool breeze that varies in pressure with each new burst of wind and I try and visualize the strands of wind as they flow over my shoulders, my face, my arms.

I allow myself time to wait and observe the air, sensing the difference in temperature, speed, direction, weight, quality, and pressure. As time passes, I notice a light buzz hanging in the air, as if it's awakening. Each gust of wind against my skin stimulates my nerves like a small electric zap.

Another current of electricity hits my body as a big gust

of wind blows into my chest. I imagine the current is made up of several threads, each thread a different color. As another burst of colorful threads hits me, they break apart and splay off in different directions. The yellow thread flows over my right shoulder and down my back and the pink flows under my ear, leaving a cool mark as it lifts my hair off my neck.

As the different colors flow over my body, I experience an overwhelming urge to dance within them. I start spinning in circles, arms stretched out wide, visualizing the colorful threads of wind circling around my body and up into the sky as I raise my arms higher.

The buzz from the air surrounding me awakens my body and I stop spinning to bask in that sensation. The gentle wind continues to rotate around me, whipping my hair around my face...

Wait.

How can I feel it rotating around me?

I open my eyes and the scene in front of me takes my breath away. I'm encapsulated within a small whirlwind. Small leaves and petals circle my body from the ground up into the sky, falling back down then joining back again at the bottom. The whirlwind ceases and slowly the debris falls to the grass, leaving the air sitting still.

I try to take a step forward, but my legs move sluggishly as black spots appear in my vision. My mind goes fuzzy and I drop to my knees, struggling to reach my arms out to protect myself as my body collapses down. Everything goes dark.

I wake with a sudden burst of vitality and inhale with a loud gasp. Vincent has his hand on my shoulder, creases of concentration across his forehead. I don't even have to guess what he's doing. His blue energy has such a different feeling to my own that I can distinguish it coursing through me immediately.

"Thanks," I say, embarrassed.

"What the hell happened? I looked up just as you were falling to the ground."

Did he see my whirlwind? I recall our earlier conversation where this is supposed to take a while and I begin to doubt what had happened.

"I think I'm a bit exhausted," I reply honestly. I'm sleeping a lot more than usual, I'm now exercising, and I'm pushing my body beyond normal limits.

"Why don't we take a break?" Vincent suggests and I begrudgingly agree. I really want to focus on my training, but with no energy I need to give my body time to recharge.

I'm automatically drawn to the water, wishing I'd brought my bikini. Vincent follows my gaze then pulls my swimsuit from his backpack.

"Where did you get that?"

"Going for a swim was the first thing I wanted to do when I came here so I packed some for you. " He seems nonchalant at the fact he's currently handling women's clothing.

Then his statement hits me and my cheeks flush. *He* packed them for me. "Uh... who packed my bag?"

"I did. Lily refused, and no one else was home. Lily stood in your doorway smiling the whole time, so I think she took great pleasure in knowing how you'd respond to me going through your room." He shrugs.

Lily!

I grab the swimwear from his hands, quicker than necessary, as I try to control the rising heat on my face. "And where do you propose I get dressed?" I ask, signaling to the open space surrounding us.

"Wherever you propose you'll go to the bathroom." He accentuates *propose* in a mocking tone. "Or I can just turn around. I promise I won't peek." He gives me a wink and I know by now my whole face is bright red.

I quickly retreat to some shrubs on the edge of the plateau. The deep blue energy within me is not only heightening the good feelings but the bad. I'm completely horrified. I try and tune out and connect with Mother Nature again, this time more as a means of calming meditation as doing so seems to keep me grounded. I regenerate as I take some deep breaths, counting down from ten. Once I'm calmer, I quickly scan my surroundings to ensure I have privacy–not that there's anyone here except Vincent–and change into my swimsuit.

I come back onto the field and Vincent has changed his shorts. I'm astounded that he changed out here in the open. He has his back turned to me and I stare at his broad muscular shoulders which taper to his waist. A blush manifests and I am thankful that he's turned around. I still can't take my eyes off him. I really need to get a grip on myself, but everything is heightened and out of my control.

He turns back and runs his gaze over my body. I grab a towel from beside his backpack and drape it over my shoulders, trying to quiet my self-consciousness. He rolls his eyes and laughs. "There's no one but me to hide from out here."

I sigh. I'm sure he's seen it all before, so I don't really have anything to worry about. The thought causes an unpleasant sensation to run through me and I quickly pull myself together before my emotions plaster across my face. I drop the towel and head straight for the water. The contrasting cool water washes my sweaty skin as I completely submerge myself. When I resurface, I float on my back and stare at the clear blue sky, just allowing myself to be present in this moment.

Something in the corner of my eye draws my attention,

and I have just enough time to brace myself as Vincent takes a running leap off an edge on the rock wall. I duck underwater to avoid being hit with the large splash, and I watch him plummet through the water followed by the delayed sound of his impact. He emerges from a cloud of bubbles as he swims toward me and we both rise for air together.

"Are you claustrophobic?" he randomly asks with a grin.

"No. Why?"

"There's a small opening behind the waterfall and I've widened the entryway so we can get in," he says enthusiastically. "Want to go check it out?"

I look to where he just jumped down from and my stomach drops.

"I promise I won't leave your side," he tries to reassure me.

Before I have a chance to object, he heads back to his backpack and places a flashlight in his pocket. He makes his way over to the base of the waterfall and motions for me to follow. Vincent goes first and manipulates the rock to create wider hand and footholds up to the opening. He makes it seem so easy and stands on the edge, waiting for me to move.

My heart races as I begin to make my way up. Every so often a gush of water rushes over me and I grip onto the wall with all the strength in my body. He calls out to me with words of encouragement, but it's mostly drowned out by the falling water.

I finally make it to the ledge which is about halfway up the rock wall. There's a gap in the falling water and I look out over the grass field. Another exceptional scene to add to the collection from this weekend. He takes my hand and guides me behind him into the cave. His warm hand sends an electric current through me. There have been two moments between us so far that have been interrupted; once when I ran my hand through his hair, and the other when his thumb brushed against the back of my hand. Neither action has really screamed out that either of us is interested, but this is the first time he's intentionally held my hand for the sake of doing so. Or perhaps he just doesn't want me to fall? I hate over-thinking everything!

As we walk farther in, he takes his flashlight out. The sound of the waterfall echoes through the cave.

"Have you been up here before?" I ask, excited about the adventure ahead.

He shakes his head and leads me deeper into the cave. The floor is damp and slippery, and I grab onto his hand tighter. As we make our way down the passage, it widens into a large opening. There are no pathways coming off, so we've reached the full depth of the cave. Our feet squelch as we move around, and I look down at the small granules that cover the floor. Vincent proceeds to shine the flashlight up and spread across the roof is a colony of bats, their movement like a vibrating sea across the ceiling. My skin crawls.

I turn around to leave but my foot slips on a rock and I fall. Vincent's quick to wrap his arm around my waist but he drops the flashlight in the process, causing a loud clang to echo through the cavern. There's a flurry of movement over-head as high-pitched squeaks overwhelm the cave, and suddenly the bats are on the move. Vincent pushes me against the wall to get out of their path as they fly by.

I hadn't intentionally held my breath, but as the sound ceases around us, I let out a long exhale. When I look up, Vincent's face is inches away from mine, our bodies pressed up against each other. I can only just see the outline of his face from the light reflecting from the flashlight on the floor.

My heart races, thumping harder and louder. His hand moves slowly up to my neck–my skin tingling where his fingers brush along my arm–and he cups the side of my face, staring deep into my eyes, unmoving, as if waiting for my response. My breathing is shallow and hurried as I press my cheek into his hand in answer, embracing his gentle touch. He leans in closer, butterflies erupting in my stomach as his lips touch mine. The electricity I felt through our hands returns in full force as his soft lips move expertly over mine, and it takes all my effort not to think about what I might be doing right or wrong, and just be in the moment.

A bat suddenly flies overhead and I instinctively duck. I chuckle. Not in an embarrassed way but releasing some of my nerves. He smiles back. Does he feel that connection between us too? With nothing left to see, we make our way back to the entrance.

As the waterfall comes into view, he takes a running leap off the edge. I race over and watch as his head emerges through the top of the water, a smile across his face. He gestures a *come here* movement with his arms and all I can do is shake my head. Everything in my body is screaming not to do it. I turn to the footholds, but they begin to disappear into the rock wall. I glare at Vincent and he's laughing, waving his arms again for me to jump.

I stand straight and consider my options. My stomach tenses as I acknowledge that I have only one. I take a quick peek over the edge to make sure there are no rocks at the bottom and walk back into the cave. I close my eyes and take a few breaths to calm my racing heart. I start counting from ten and when I reach one, I open my eyes, swallow back any fear, and take a running jump off the edge. I scream all the way down even though it's completely exhilarating. I straighten my body just before it hits the water, then resist against the force dragging me deep underwater as I attempt to swim toward the surface.

Vincent is already beside me as I break through the top of the water. My heart is still galloping, and I take long deep breaths as I bask in the fact that I'm still alive. I give him another glare and splash him with water. *How dare he force me to jump down!* I try to show annoyance, but I can't hide the fact I'm full of adrenaline. We start swimming to the bank but as we reach a point where we can stand, he grabs my arm, turns me around and presses his lips into mine.

My mind gives me one second to get lost in his embrace, but the intensity of his movements brings back the gnawing thoughts from earlier about how this wouldn't be something new for him, whereas it's completely new to me. I can't seem to make my mind stop and I pull away from Vincent. My emotions don't seem to belong to me. Everything is raw and heightened and it makes me wonder if I would be captivated by Vincent in the same way if I had clarity of mind and emotion.

Vincent stares at me, but he doesn't speak. I can't tell if he's offended, or unfazed about my response.

He rubs the back of his neck. "We should probably head back. I've got some errands I need to get to."

He wades out of the water and walks away before I get a chance to say anything.

We make our way downhill and I find myself too breathless to talk. Not that I'd know where to start with conversation right now.

"I really appreciate everything you've done for me this weekend," I finally manage to say once we've almost reached the cabin.

"We need to do what it takes to keep each other safe. I don't know if you can feel it yet, but there's a purpose to what we can accomplish. Why else would our ancestors have continued the line for almost four centuries? It may not be during our lifetime, but there will be a reason we persisted against all odds."

I don't know how to respond. Everything is so new that I don't sense this purpose he's talking about which makes me feel inadequate.

He keeps on walking.

CHAPTER EIGHT

As the cabin comes into view, there's a familiar car parked in the driveway and my stomach drops. Lily or Aunt Amy is here.

Vincent notices my hesitation and walks with me inside.

"Hi, Kaylee," my mother says, and I stop dead in the doorway.

I knew I was going to have to address my mother soon, and I thought I was ready, but I haven't had enough time to process it all. Suddenly, all the anger I've been suppressing this weekend emerges. I'm so angry that my whole life has been a lie. The thought of asking why I couldn't be trusted sends a wave of sadness through me. Even Lily was trusted with the information.

I open my mouth to speak but no sound comes out. She senses my hesitation and takes a step toward me. As she moves closer the cabin feels smaller and smaller. Every fiber of my being wants to turn around and walk right away from her. My whole life I've never been able to do what I want and that needs to stop now, so I listen to what my body is telling me, and I walk away.

"Kaylee!" Mom calls after me but I don't stop. She catches up to me in the clearing and grabs me by the wrist. "Please, stop."

I look up at her, tears threatening to spill. "No! You stop! Stop pretending like you give a damn about me!" The hurt, the rage, it all pours out of me with words I know are going to hurt her, but right now I want her to feel just a sliver of the anguish that is coursing through me.

She looks at me sternly. "Until you have a child of your own, you don't know what it's like to want to do everything in your power to keep them safe."

"Safe from what, Mom? Safe from not being able to make friends? Yep, that sure didn't happen with all the moving around. Safe from boys? Those two chaperones I've had my whole life do a rather good job of that. Safe from graduations, birthday parties, my freedom?" It all pours out of me and I can't seem to stop. My whole life I've worked so hard to suppress my anguish toward our lifestyle because there was nothing that I could do to change it, but now, after experiencing this freedom, I realize what I've missed out on and I'm excruciatingly angry.

Wind whirls around us and I wonder if my emotions are causing a reaction when Mom steps back from me, arms outstretched. The wind picks up speed, and debris on the ground starts swirling around her. As each second passes the whirlwind grows with intensity and soon the sound of the whirling is all I can hear. It's so strong I have to fight against the pressure pulling me into the now tornado.

And as quickly as it had emerged, the tornado dissipates and the air hangs still around us.

Her chest heaves up and down as she steadies her breathing. Her anger is palpable. "This power we have isn't a game, Kaylee. It is a weapon. To defend and attack. Is this the sort of life you want to become involved in?" She looks at Vincent and stretches her hand toward him. His knees give way as he clutches his throat, mouth open, gaping, but no sound coming out. "Do you still feel you're missing out on something?" she yells at me.

"Mom, stop!" I scream at her.

Vincent slams his hand into the ground and a mound of earth rises underneath Mom's feet. She loses her focus as she rises over ten feet in the air and Vincent takes a large breath. He throws his hands forward and a ball of dirt shoots in her direction. She dives off the side of the mound and I gasp, knowing she's going to break something when she hits the ground. But a large gust of wind passes by me as she gracefully glides forward, then rights herself and takes a casual step that lands her feet back on the ground.

Vincent takes aim again, but I step in his way, holding my arms out to both of them. My head is spinning.

"What the hell, Maria?" Vincent yells at my mother.

"You were out of line!" she responds firmly, and I know she's talking about me.

"She almost exposed us. You should be thanking me for being there to cover it up."

Mom stares at him, her brow furrowed, then her shoulders drop. "It wasn't supposed to go like this." Gone is her anger, now replaced by anguish. She turns to me. "I was meant to be the one to tell you when the time was right. Everything I've done, I've done to protect you."

I intentionally roll my eyes. "Trust me, Mom, with the number of people who remind me that you're just being protective, I won't be forgetting it anytime soon." My voice is laced with a mocking tone and I don't try to hide it. And because she chose this life of secrecy for me, it's meant a life of absolutely no freedom, with no explanation of why. I've grown to resent her so much, and maybe if she'd trusted me, our relationship may not be as broken as it is now.

I'm expecting her to be angry following my outburst, but she turns to Vincent. "She doesn't know yet, does she?"

His gaze drops and he shakes his head.

I'm so sick of half-truths. "Someone please tell me what's going on," I shout.

"I'm not in the army, Kaylee," my mother answers. "You have no idea how hard it's been for me to miss out on watching you grow up, but I wouldn't change a second of it. Our kind is not safe, and I have done everything in my power to keep that from you, and I would do it all again."

"What do you mean our kind isn't safe?"

She lets out a long exhale. "When the witch-hunts ended, the people at the forefront of the killings knew there were still those with powers among them. Full of jealousy and self-righteousness, they formulated their own secret organization called XET."

"XET?" I ask, repeating each letter. I've never heard of such an organization.

"Based on the three men who formed the group: Xtopher, Edward and Thomas. XET's only purpose is to eradicate our kind. We managed to escape them for a few generations, but ever since the early nineteen-hundreds, they've been solely targeting our lineage. The reason we move around so often is because we can't risk being in one place for too long."

We move so much because of XET? So, Aunt Amy is choosing different jobs because of our safety, not because she wants to? I really was the only one left out.

"You might think that being privy to this information might have made your childhood a lot easier, but imagine growing up knowing there are people out there who are trying to track you down and kill you." She looks at me dead in the eyes to make sure I understand. "My job for the last fourteen years has been to track XET and I won't stop until the people who want to hurt us–but more importantly, the people who want to hurt you–are gone." Her voice catches as she says the last part.

There are people out there that want to kill me? The thought repeatedly runs through my head and the hairs on my arms stand as the temperature drops. I rub my arms to try and warm myself up, and I find my mind wandering into a vicious cycle of *what ifs*. My breathing accelerates and my hands continue their repetitive motion of rubbing up and down, up and down.

A warmth over my hands halts my movement, and I look up into Vincent's deep blue eyes. He doesn't speak; it's just a silent reminder that he's there. He's been there every time I've needed him this weekend.

I chastise myself. How could I be so stupid... thinking that I'm only captivated by him because my emotions are in turmoil. How could I not care about someone who has been nothing but kind, honest and accepting of everything I am?

I take a deep breath and the fresh scent of the surroundings stabilizes me in the moment. My hands relax down to my sides, but Vincent still has a gentle hold of one of them.

Mom is staring at the two of us and I quickly let go of his hand. Her handbag is open, and I know she was trying to find my spare medication. She always comes prepared although my anxiety usually isn't this persistent. I've had more anxiety attacks in the last three days than I have in the last year but I'm ecstatic that I haven't had to take my medication for it. While feeling uncontrolled in a panic attack is a horrible feeling, at least I feel something. The medication they've prescribed makes me feel nothing at all. I literally sit there for hours with an empty mind.

She wanted to protect me from this threat, but years of isolation and constantly being the new kid have made an impact on my mental wellbeing. It makes sense why Vincent went out of his way to find me. I basically activated a massive beacon the other night that said I'm not normal. What if I've done something to lead XET to us? I'd never forgive myself. I need to learn better coping skills for my anxiety and to control my gifts, otherwise I'm a risk to us all.

I look up at Mom, not yet sure what to say in response.

"Will you come home now?" she asks.

I make direct eye contact. Now is the opportunity to stand up for myself. "No. I'm not ready yet." I don't want to argue with her anymore, but I need more time. "If it's okay with Pop and Vincent, I'd like to stay here..." I can see her hesitation. "This life is new to me and I'm not about to put it aside and forget that it exists, Mom. I need time to focus on myself for once. If you take me home, I'll find a way to train anyway, but there'll be so much more risk of exposure or hurting someone."

She sighs deeply. "I never wanted you involved in this life. Not yet. I knew eventually I'd divulge the truth, but I had hoped that XET would no longer be a threat to you when that happened."

I shake my head. "But they are and right now the best thing I can do for myself, for everyone, is to train."

She rubs her hands over her face, obviously frustrated, but I think she's beginning to accept that she can't keep me away from this any longer. "Air is a powerful force, Kaylee. It's invisible, yet it can be used defensively or as an attack. It completely surrounds us and is within us. Without air, we could not survive." She looks sympathetically at Vincent and apologizes for her earlier outburst.

"What did you do to Vincent?" I ask, genuinely intrigued.

"When Vincent moves earth, the empty space where the earth came from is replaced by air. But if we shift air, it isn't necessarily replaced by more air. Like sucking the last bit of air out of a balloon, if you empty out a vessel, say the lungs, it can create a vacuum. If you don't allow air back in to fill up the lungs, it renders the user unable to breathe. But you must be extremely cautious. Depriving a body of oxygen will initially cause fainting, but it can cause brain damage leading to comas or even death, and if you release the air back into the lungs too quickly it can cause irreversible damage.

"As much as I hate the idea of you training, I won't stop you. Now that you've accessed your gift it's important you learn how to keep it under control. I understand that you're trying to figure everything out, but just remember you have a family waiting for you, who have gone to extreme lengths to keep you safe."

I need more time before I can get anywhere remotely close to understanding the lies, but I give her a small nod in acknowledgment.

"How long are you staying?" I ask, hopeful that we can have some training time together.

"I need to leave soon but I can stay for dinner?"

Is she asking me for permission to stay? "No more secrets." My throat tightens as the words come out. The pain is still so raw.

"No more secrets," she confirms.

I nod in response to her statement, but also to her earlier question of staying for dinner.

The afternoon passes quickly as Pop, Vincent, Mom, and I prepare for dinner. Before I have a chance to think about any other dire questions, we've finished eating and I find myself struggling to keep my eyes open. Today has been yet another day full of an overwhelming amount of information.

As we sit around the fireplace talking, I sink deeper into the cushions, my eyelids getting heavier.

A sudden intensity of heat under my feet stirs me awake. How long have I been asleep? Mom's hushed voice beside me alerts me enough to keep my eyes shut, but I slowly wriggle my feet away from the fire. The whispering stops, but I must be putting on a good performance, as they continue talking moments later.

"We lost Cody last month," Mom says solemnly.

"That means Shailie is the last negative water?" Pop sounds shocked.

His statement confuses me, but I don't have time to get caught up on the details, otherwise I'll miss the conversation.

"Yes, now there's three of us down to the last generation," Mom reconfirms.

There's silence for another minute.

"So, what's the plan from here?" Vincent asks.

I almost open my eyes at the realization he's being involved. This conversation could have occurred over dinner, but it feels as though they've specifically waited for me to not be present. Especially since they stopped talking when I stirred. My gut tenses at the thought of Vincent trying to hide information from me.

"Now Shailie is the last of her line, we can't risk her fighting among us. There's only a handful of us out there in the field so we're only making small gains. It's getting harder to keep an eye on them now our numbers are dwindling."

"I should be out there with you," Pop interrupts furiously.

"No!" Mom quickly reacts, then lowers her voice to a whisper again. "I need you here protecting them. We can't have our eyes everywhere, so I need the reassurance you'll be here." Her voice is pleading.

"You know I'll protect her with my life," Pop says without hesitation.

My mouth is suddenly dry as I realize the magnitude of his statement. The magnitude of the situation. XET are closing in, and Mom is risking everything.

"I really hope it doesn't come to that. We tracked XET in Charlotte last week so please keep your eyes and ears open."

I almost make a noise. That's only a few hours from here.

Mom continues. "Their movement has stopped completely in the last two days so we're keeping a close eye on them to ensure they're not planning on sticking around this area."

My stomach tightens. I need to learn to control my gift and defend myself. XET are too close.

"On that note, I really should get back to work."

A gentle hand runs through my hair and I allow my eyes to slowly open. Mom looks down at me with a smile.

"I've got to go."

I wrap my arms around her. For the first time, I'm afraid of saying goodbye. I'd always thought she was going away to warzones, but as I'd understood, it was never her job to be on the front line. XET are more real and dangerous than I could imagine.

She turns to leave but adds in, "School tomorrow, be there or I'll be back to drag you there myself."

I groan. School has been the last thing on my mind.

"You have no idea how valuable knowledge can be. Being one of the active eight can be all-encompassing, but you have a life outside of it where you're going to go to college, get a job and be a part of society. Promise me you'll go?"

"Okay," I reply, reminding myself there's only a week left before the summer break.

I'm sure I can manage that. I never promised anything about next year.

I watch until she drives out of sight, then I excuse myself to the bedroom. Right now, I just want to be on my own. I make another mental note to add *active eight* to my ever-growing list of questions for Vincent.

I use the time alone to shower and prepare for school. Despite having a bag full of clothes, I dig out Vincent's shirt and welcome the soft material against my skin.

As I lie down, I think about Mom's request. I honestly don't understand how she can expect me to see school as a priority when my life has completely changed. I shouldn't be sitting in a room all day, multiplying numbers, and writing short stories. I should be out here training, turning myself into a weapon.

I lie back on the bed as my fury grows deeper about the life XET has forced us to lead. I will make it my mission to follow in my mom's footsteps.

I toss and turn for what feels like hours before a restless night's sleep takes hold.

CHAPTER NINE

I jolt as I'm awoken by strong hands shaking my shoulders. I attempt to sit up, trying to focus as the morning sun invades my vision, but as I try to move, my legs seize and refuse to cooperate. If that's the result of one hike, I don't even want to imagine how I'm going to feel after all the other training.

"Sorry, you weren't answering when I knocked," Vincent says.

The fog slowly lifts as my mind attempts to register where I am and what day it is.

"I've been working on Pop's Jeep to get it ready for you to get to school, but I just need a touch more time. I thought you'd want some time to get ready in the meantime."

I groan. *School.*

I rub my face, then let out a yawn. "Thanks." It's all I can manage to say as the exhaustion refuses to be lifted.

He turns around to leave but pauses and looks me up and down. "Nice shirt. It suits you."

And just like that, I'm completely awake as my face flushes with embarrassment. I lie back on the bed and cover my face with a pillow, wishing the bed would suck me out of this world.

This world that is no longer safe.

And I'm putting us all at risk.

My stomach tenses as I recall last night's conversation. My mother is risking her life trying to keep me safe, so I need to give everything I have to control my power to avoid exposing us all, and learn to use it as a weapon so that I can defend myself against XET.

My thoughts move me into action and I quickly get ready for school and take the small amount of free time to train. I don't bother wasting time eating. I figure I'll be able to skip breakfast through regenerating.

Yesterday I created my first whirlwind, although I'm not convinced it actually happened. I quickly regenerate, then focus on connecting to air.

Within seconds the air buzzes around me. Vincent said accessing the element would be the easy part and it seems I've unlocked that door.

A gust of wind comes past me and I reach out and catch it. My whole body radiates as I project my energy into the wind and spiral it around my feet and up into the air.

My hair whips around my face as a whirlwind encases me and I forcefully project my energy out to try to keep the momentum moving as I count. *Five seconds, ten seconds, fifteen seconds.* My body sways and I immediately release my hold. Yesterday's fainting episode has taught me a lesson.

I throw my hands out wide and raise my face to the sky, opening my body up to Mother Nature. I thrive on the energy that's entering, but it flows in slower than usual.

I take a step, but my body staggers and my knees hit the ground.

"Come child," a gentle voice calls from behind me, "you need to eat something."

I turn around to Pop's outstretched hand. As I grab hold, he opens a channel and passes energy along. The magnitude of energy available within him overwhelms me, but before I have a chance to think any further, he quickly removes his hand. Even though it was a brief encounter, a large amount of gray-blue energy–a mixture of his blue eyes and a gray to show his age–whirls throughout my body. I don't know why, but envisioning colors when I feel the exchange helps me to understand the process behind what we can do, which allows me to control it better.

He takes me inside and leads me to the kitchen. It's a small kitchen, lined with waist high benches and large cabinets across the back wall. There's a gas stove on the bench beside the sink. The bench is L-shaped, running along one wall but jutting out to section it off from the living room. There are wooden stools pulled up to the bench, and they're just as exquisite as the rest of the wooden furniture in the cabin. No microwave, no fridge, no dishwasher.

"How do you keep food fresh?" I ask curiously.

"When you can control earth, it makes finding fresh food very simple." He motions out the kitchen window and I stare out into a large garden abundant with fruits and vegetables. "Otherwise, I go hunting for most of my meat and dry it out, so it doesn't need to be cooled. All the other items are canned or packet food. There's no power here so we don't have the luxuries of the modern times."

He makes some eggs and beans, with a side of jerky, and sets the plate in front of me. My stomach groans in anticipation as the smell filters through my body.

"Thank you," I say through a mouthful of food. "Pop... can you tell me more about XET?" The only thing I'm working toward is making sure I'm not a liability because I'd never forgive myself if I drew XET here, or if I couldn't protect myself from them.

"They used to be a much larger group, but as witches started being turned into fables their credibility declined, and through the efforts of your mother and the others who are chasing them, they have dwindled to just two families. Their children have been born in an environment where they're taught to fear and hate us, and this has made the last few generations extremely dangerous.

"Unfortunately, when the witch hunts ceased, a lot of organizations continued to secretly fund XET which gave them enough income to set up a home base that's protected beyond our capabilities. We haven't been able to target them there, so can only find them when they're out looking for us. They're extremely cunning and patient though. They know how dangerous we can be so they plan for weeks, months even, then will suddenly attack and we lose another of us."

"What exactly do you do to them once you find them?" I'm dreading the answer, but I have to know what I'm in for.

"If safe to do so, we try to capture them before eliminating them to gather any information, but if not, then the orders are to kill." When he sees me flinch, he adds in, "We could have a long and fulfilling life, but most of our kind are lucky to get beyond fifty years because of XET. The fact that I'm still around is a testament to the work that your mom has been doing. My daughter wasn't so lucky. Both she and her partner died protecting Vincent and Tyler so they could escape."

My stomach drops at the thought that I might be a third of the way through my life, but even more at the fact that Vincent lost his parents to these people.

"Tyler?"

A familiar voice speaks up from behind me. "A younger, not as smart or good-looking, version of me," Vincent jibes, wiping his greasy hands on a cloth. "He's my brother."

A younger brother? There's so much I don't know about Vincent.

"Does he control the earth element too?" I ask curiously.

Vincent chuckles. "He wishes he was that cool. He controls water."

I look at him, confused. If Vincent can control earth, how can a relation control another element?

"I have... had," he corrects himself solemnly, "two mothers. Mom and Momma both descended from the women with whom Charlotte–the original witch–shared her powers. Tyler and I both have the same donor father but different mothers, and therefore the different element control."

It makes me furious that XET are responsible for the deaths of Vincent and Tyler's mothers. It stirs something deep inside me. Before I can continue the conversation, Vincent's alarm goes off.

"Time to go."

I thank Pop for breakfast and follow Vincent outside. I head toward his pickup, but he leads me around the side of the house to another vehicle. I recall him talking about a Jeep this morning, but I was too tired to register.

"It's old and creaky, but it runs. You can use it to get to and from school."

"Thank you, Vincent, I really appreciate that." Honestly, Vincent has gone beyond necessary to accommodate me being here. "But I don't think I can remember the way out of the forest."

"You can follow me out. We'll stop somewhere close to your school," he offers.

Vincent gets in his pickup and I follow closely, trying to pay attention to landmarks as we make our way out. It takes just under an hour before we're out of the forest and close to Highway 25. Vincent pulls over in front of a Starbucks and my body rejoices at the thought of fresh coffee.

"Keep following this road north and it'll take you straight to your school. I'll meet you back here around four?" he says through my window.

"That sounds great, thanks."

It's already past 8:00 so I decide to go straight to school, after a quick stop to buy a coffee. My mind starts wandering to Lily and for the first time I'm not sure how to react around her. It feels as if we've been apart for months. We were always close as children, but everything started changing in high school. Aunt Amy had said that she was just hormonal and to give her space, but we were never close again. Is that when she found out about my secret? Or has she known her whole life?

As I make my way along the highway, the majestic brick building comes into view. I've always been astonished by the design of Asheville High School. To me it looks more like a palace with its tower in the center and long buildings extending off to each side.

I find a park at the back of the lot and make my way inside. The quiet of the hallways confuses me. Usually they're filled with students buzzing around but everyone is lined up in front of their classes with their heads in their books or talking quietly. It takes a moment to register what I'm seeing, but once I realize, my stomach drops. *Exams!*

I rummage through my backpack to try and find my timetable and race to my English classroom. Mrs. Jordan has just started bringing the students into the room, so I quickly join the end of the line and try to shift my line of thinking into exam mode.

I walk past Lily on my way to a seat, but she doesn't look at me. Right now, I don't have time to worry about her, so I turn my attention to the back of the exam paper on my desk. As I sit waiting, an odd sensation runs through me as if to say *what am I doing here*?

Mrs. Jordan announces that the exam has begun and the sound of exam papers turning over fills the silence. I flip my own paper over and stare at the task: write a 1000-word short story within the outlined set of restrictions. *I'm so glad I'm here and not training because my ability to spell and write is going to come in so handy when I'm faced with XET.* I roll my eyes as I listen to the sarcastic voice inside my head, but I finally face the fact that I promised Mom I'd be here. I start writing my story.

It surprised me how nice it was to escape for the last two hours as I cultivated a story set in an alternate world. No worrying about the mundane life I no longer have, or the new life I'm yet to establish.

As we're herded out of the room, I call after Lily. I need some answers before I can try to move past everything that has happened. She stops momentarily for me to catch up and we make our way to the cafeteria.

With so many people around, I must be incredibly careful about my word choice. She isn't saying anything, so I decide to start with the basics.

"How are you?" I ask.

"Great," she replies shortly.

Silence.

"How was your weekend?" I try again.

"Great," she repeats, sounding just as snippy.

Her attitude makes me frustrated. What does she have to

be angry about anyway? I'm the one whose life has been a complete lie.

"I thought you'd be a bit happier now you don't need to chaperone me and there's no more secrets?" I sound harsher than I meant.

"Of course, because now that you know, it means everything about the last few years can be wiped away. Poor Kaylee, who had been given a perfect life without having to worry about a thing. Disregard the fact that everyone around her worked so damn hard to give her that perfect life at the expense of their own happiness."

People are starting to stop and stare as Lily lets loose on me. I grab her by the arm to try and take her outside to talk but an intense heat radiates under my hand and I flinch at the sudden pain. A small blister begins to form on the edge of my palm.

"Don't you dare touch me," Lily shouts furiously. "Just because we're paired doesn't mean we have to get along."

There's so much going on that I don't understand, but I can't stand by while she offends me. "Well, you don't have to worry about seeing me anytime soon because I won't be returning home in a hurry."

"Of course, because everyone has to accommodate what Kaylee wants. She has a tantrum and runs away without understanding the repercussions. Well this time it's not just my life you're ruining but Tyler's too."

This time I can't hide my confusion. What does Vincent's brother have to do with this?

"You're still so utterly clueless. I guess dear Vincent hasn't told you everything."

All the hurt from being lied to my whole life resurfaces at the thought that Vincent still hasn't been completely honest either. Even last night he was talking about XET behind my back.

Right now, I can't stand the sight of Lily. Plus, I can tell nothing I say will change her current mood and I'm only putting myself in the firing line by sticking around so I turn around and walk away from her. I'm so furious at her, and Vincent, and everything about this last week, that I just continue to walk.

Eventually the hallway ends, and I find myself at one of the exits of the school. I look over the vast cascade of stairs that lead up to the building. It would be so simple to just walk out and never turn back. There is absolutely no doubt in my mind that this will be the last week of schooling I ever attend. I'm not going to learn anything this week either as it's just exams, so there really isn't any point dragging this out any further.

I begrudgingly remember my promise to Mom and let out a long sigh. I've always liked to think that my word meant something, and right now breaking that promise goes against every grain in my body. I will do this for her. One last week.

I've missed my opportunity to have lunch, but happily remember that food doesn't always matter anymore. I quickly regenerate. I head to my next exam fully aware I'll be earlier than necessary, but I know Lily isn't in the next class so I will be safe from seeing her again. I'm not sure how I'll react if I confront her again today.

Thanks to a half-hearted attempt to complete the exam, I'm packed and ready to go as soon as the bell rings. It ends up being a good decision to leave straight away as by the time I exit the parking lot, I only just end up getting to Vincent on time. I've rarely been out without Mom, Lily or Aunt Amy, so I've never needed a cell phone, but I'm starting to think it might be time. I make a mental note to tell Vincent I'll be late tomorrow afternoon, so I'll have time to buy one.

I don't get out of the car to greet him, just beep the horn as I'm driving past to let him know I'm happy to lead. I'm trying to figure out what I'm going to say to Vincent, but right now the fury deep inside me won't let me think clearly. Despite that, I manage to take all the correct turns but one. It helps that there aren't a lot of turns. The final road to Pop's doesn't seem to be on the map I found in his Jeep, but I imagine he and Vincent may have had a hand in creating the dirt road.

I step out of the car and make my way to Vincent, certain that my rage is going to burst, but I startle myself as a quiet, somber voice escapes. "I thought I could trust you to tell me the truth."

Vincent has the audacity to look confused.

"Lily told me that me being here affects Tyler and you knew about it? And I've heard three people now speak about something called *paired*? And last night you were all talking about XET after I'd fallen asleep."

His face softens. "I swear I wasn't keeping the truth from you. It might not feel like it, but I was going to explain the rest this week. There's so much to take in about our history, then when your mom showed up and told you about XET, I figured you had enough to think about already."

"Why couldn't you just tell me there was more and that we could talk about it later?"

He raises his eyebrows. "Do you really think you would have waited to talk about it later?"

I think about it for a quick second but shake my head in defeat. No, I would have insisted he told me then and there.

"Why don't you pack a bag and we'll head up to the

plateau for the afternoon? There's still a few hours left of light and we can talk on the way up."

Right now, training is my priority, so I agree to his proposal. I figure the hike is good for my stamina too, rather than just staying here to train.

I quickly gather a few things together–this time collecting my own swimsuit just in case–and we begin the journey to the plateau.

CHAPTER TEN

Vincent walks ahead of me again, and he doesn't respond for a while. I can only presume he's trying to gather his thoughts.

"I've already told you about Charlotte, but there's more to her story. When Charlotte was completing the ritual to pass on her gifts, she was rushed by the witch hunters and we can only guess that something went wrong because nine months later each woman birthed not one, but two babies each. Twins."

I turn to Vincent, not understanding why having twins would be seen as wrong. "So, Charlotte's power was passed on to eight children, rather than four? Why would that be an issue? You said she feared her gifts leaving the Earth, but maybe she meant for twins to double the certainty of her power remaining?"

Vincent chuckles as he shakes his head. "I don't know why I was worried about overloading you with information. You're keeping up just fine. We don't believe Charlotte meant for twins because even though each set of twins inherited the ability to control one of the elements, they soon realized something strange was happening. Whenever a set of twins was separated, anyone in the nearby vicinity of the children started behaving differently."

"What do you mean they behaved differently?" I quickly cut him off, imagining people randomly breaking out in shameful dance moves or talking in an accent.

"Basically, they started acting out of norm for their personality. Actions such as taking up drinking alcohol or smoking or being overly friendly and volunteering all their spare time to help friends and neighbors.

"No one could figure out why this whole town would have fleeting moments where people's behavior changed until a whole street had been affected over the period of a week. One of the children went away hunting with his father and by the time they returned, the mother–who had been left with the other sibling–and their close neighbors had fallen into disarray. They stopped working, weren't looking after themselves, and had fallen into a deep depression. As soon as the child and his father returned, it was as if a fog had been lifted and everyone went back to normal, as if nothing had happened.

"On the other hand, the father–who was only supposed to go away for one night–explained that he hadn't caught anything but was suddenly overwhelmed with this desperate need to provide for his family. He refused to stop until he caught something. It was the child begging to return to his mother that eventually saw the father returning.

"The parents sat down and tried to recall all the times they'd had this fog over their eyes and eventually realized it was while they were alone with one of the children.

"The families of the eight children gathered, and all were able to identify similar stories. One of each twin-set seemed to make people behave positively, and the other influenced negative choices. But only when they were separated. Like two sides of a magnet, it seemed they had this influence expel from them whenever they were separated that called out to their other half to try and reconnect them. When apart, they were continuously active and sending out impulses, but together they were calm and neutralized."

Vincent gives me a moment and I try to collect my thoughts. "Do you think there's a purpose to this influence they emit?"

"My guess is that the twins were never meant to be two separate people, and it's basically her power calling out to itself to try and keep together."

"So, what does this have to do with paired?" That was my original question and he hasn't used the word once.

"When the twins started having children of their own, the babies also had this influence. If their mother could control water, and influenced people positively, then so did the child. Through the generations we've been able to minimize our effect on other people by pairing off a negative person to a positive person. Fortunately, we're only able to have one child each so it's much easier to keep everyone paired off."

I stare at him with wide eyes. "What do you mean we can only have one child?"

"Once the power is passed along to a child, we become infertile. The only time anyone has been able to have more is sadly after the death of their child. It's as if the parent reactivates to be able to continue the line," he says it all as if it's another fact in everyday life.

Vincent has known all his life that this was how his world works, so his detachment from emotion shouldn't surprise me, but for me it's much more emotional. I've always known I wanted to have children but now being told I'm being limited to one makes me yearn for the big family I'll never have. Sure, there might be alternative options like adoption, but would I really want to knowingly bring a child into this world?

I rub my arm–a nervous habit I've developed over time– and my palm stings. I look at my hand and consider Vincent's previous statements.

"Today, Lily said I was her pair."

"She is. You're a positive air, and Lily is a negative fire. You, Lily, Tyler and I make up four of the current active eight."

So, Lily knows about this because she's one of us? She had been so hot to touch today. That must have been her fire usage. Vincent also just called me a positive air... And he mentioned active eight again... I groan. I have so many questions.

"Active eight?" I look at him, confused, starting with the simplest of my questions.

"It refers to the youngest generation of element users. There's two who control water, two fire, two earth and two air."

"And this influence, how does it work?"

"You've probably never noticed because you've been so closely guarded by Lily."

He could say that again! After the talk with Mom I thought the reason I've always been chaperoned is because of my safety against XET, but now I'm realizing it's also to do with stopping me from affecting people.

"When you're initially separated from Lily, your positive impact would only be very minor on the people around you. Something simple such as choosing a piece of fruit over junk food for example. The more time you're apart, the more the force strengthens and the choices and actions of the people around you would become more dramatic. Eventually they would only spend their time on work or study commitments, helping with charities or teaching people less fortunate. That may not sound like such a bad thing, but the problem is these people start neglecting themselves as they basically work or starve themselves to death.

"On the other side of the spectrum, those around Lily in the beginning might just do something simple as having another drink at the pub, but over time this turns into an addiction with drugs, refusing to work, and committing crimes. Eventually they may overdose, become homeless or end up in prison.

"When you reconnect, your influence subsides on those around you and they go back to being themselves, but once you separate again the cycle recommences."

"And there's nothing I can do to control it?"

"Not unless you keep yourself by the side of a negative element user for the rest of your life. Which is why Tyler has become involved with you being here. Because you and I have basically been paired all weekend, Tyler has been staying at Lily's to reduce the energy field that was building around them both."

There are so many emotions running through me. Guilt first for Tyler, and Lily if I'm being honest. Because I'm staying here, they've had to rearrange their lives. Then anger. So much anger. I've basically just been told my life is no longer mine, it's part of another half. A simple choice to have a weekend away would involve so many other people and factors. And it's something I'm going to have to consider for the rest of my life by the sound of it. How does that even work? Must we live in the same household for the rest of our lives or can we be neighbors? Do we have to work in the same building? The thought of being able to influence people to make choices that aren't their own makes me nauseous. And then there's the sadness. Having to now process what my future family dynamic might look like.

I've been so engrossed in our conversation that I hadn't noticed we'd arrived at the plateau. With no more revelations from Vincent, he delves straight into training. I attempt to regenerate but my mind is so frazzled that it's hard to think straight. I look around at my surroundings but don't see–or feel–that golden energy.

"I'm sorry," I say, defeated. "I can't focus enough to regenerate right now."

"If you ever find yourself faced with XET, the last thing on your mind is going to be the harmonious connection with Mother Nature. But that's the one thing you will be relying on to fuel your element. Use this as a learning exercise to overcome what's getting in your way to regenerate."

I'm so mentally exhausted right now that I just want to turn around and go back to the cabin, but I think about the truth in his words. I need to be able to regenerate under pressure.

"How do you regenerate when you can't even sense the energy?"

"You answered your own question before. You said you couldn't focus enough. Try focusing."

I roll my eyes at him. I know I need to concentrate, but that involves getting past all the other thoughts. This feels like the same situation I get stuck in with my anxiety attacks. I get so caught up in my thoughts that I can't concentrate. I try a few deep mindful breaths, zoning in on the sensation of the air coming in and out of my lungs, letting any other thoughts flow straight through me. It takes a minute but finally, with my focus redirected, I begin to sense that familiar golden glow around me. I quickly take the moment to regenerate.

"So now that we know you can get past that, do you want to talk about what's going through your mind?" Vincent asks.

I sigh. "There's just been a lot to take in this week." Everything about this whole lifestyle is so complex, irrespective of XET. For a fraction of a second, I can understand why Mom has tried to keep me away.

"What's your biggest fear?" Vincent asks.

"XET. Being responsible for leading them to us and not being able to defend myself against them. And unintentionally hurting someone from not being able to control air properly, or through giving off that positive influence for too long."

He pauses for a second. "The positive influence is something that's beyond your control, apart from remaining paired with Lily. Considering that's something we can't change, why don't we focus on controlling your element. Once you've done that then you won't feel like such a threat of exposing us when you're around other people, and it will give you the defenses you need if you're ever faced with XET."

His words resonate with me. My focus needs to be on element training as it's the one thing I have control over right now, and my biggest disadvantage. With clarity of mind, I look at Vincent, eager to start.

"Why don't you start with trying to connect to your element again?"

I shift my gaze to my feet and decide to answer honestly. "I think I already have." I've been attempting numerous times today to connect to air when I had free time at school, and every time I could immediately sense the air around me. Unable to act on the sensation, I used the time to sit back and assess. The change in the feel of it around people when they inhaled compared to when they exhaled. The movement of the wind circulating from the fan overhead. The freshness of the air flowing into the room through an open window.

Just the thought about connecting to air right now has my surroundings vibrating.

"Well, why don't you show me what you can do with that connection," Vincent asks with eyebrows raised. A challenge.

I focus on the different threads of wind flowing over my body and continue from where I left off this morning. I catch one of the strands and command it to alter its course to rotate around my feet, and slowly wind its way up my body. I circle thread after thread around my feet as I grasp more strands of wind as they flow toward me.

I keep my eyes locked on Vincent, wanting to prove my worth. My whirlwind gains enough strength that small bits of debris float up and around me.

My knees begin to buckle as the golden energy dwindles inside me. I've made the mistake too many times to completely deplete my supply and quickly cut off my connection to the whirlwind. It takes a moment for the wind to dissipate, but eventually the dirt and debris drift down gently to the ground.

Vincent continues to stare at me, and I don't think he's going to say or do anything for a good while. I usually shy away from standing out, but this time I stand up a little taller and embrace my achievement. I give him a nervous smile.

"That was incredible," he finally manages to blurt out. "That's no small feat to control your element so well already!"

I blush slightly. "I created a whirlwind yesterday. I think that's why I passed out as I didn't stop myself in time before my energy ran out. Mind you, it felt stronger today and I managed to preserve some energy." I'm feeling extremely proud of myself and I'm sure it's showing on my face. I'm waiting for Vincent to reciprocate my feelings, but he just stands there, looking perplexed.

"Isn't this a good thing?" I question, sounding slightly more hurt than I intended.

"Yes, of course!" he quickly confirms. "I think I'm just a bit stunned. Maybe a bit envious even. I think you've bruised my ego." He adds in the last bit with a chuckle. "Do you have enough left in the tank to try again?"

I shake my head. "I don't think I'll be up for more for a little while."

He motions to the water. "Why don't we enjoy the afternoon then?"

He's got another thing coming if he thinks I'm going to be jumping off any ledges again!

After quickly changing, I walk to the water's edge to dip my toes in and test the temperature. As I put my foot down all I feel is a lump of dirt. I shake my head, thinking how strange that was, and try a different spot and the same thing happens.

Vincent chuckles. He's using his earth skills against me! I turn around and give him my dirtiest stare which only spurs him on, and he breaks down into fits of laughter. *Glad he's finding this so amusing. I swear once I control air then he won't see the end of it.* I turn back around and try to step in the water, paying so much attention to the shoreline that I miss Vincent bolting toward me. He picks me up quicker than I can respond and we both fly into the water.

I wriggle out of his grasp and find my footing then splash him with water. It takes him off-guard and he laughs then splashes back twice as much. Suddenly a water fight breaks out and for the first time I completely let my defenses down and the happiness that creeps in is exhilarating.

As I try to run to the bank, Vincent manipulates the mud to build up and over my feet, encompassing them. I try to lift my leg, but it won't budge. He charges toward me again and tackles me down but this time we land near the bank on a section of soft mud. I grab a handful of dirt and smear it over his chest, my heart racing as my hand moves over the definition of his muscles.

He responds with a cheeky smile then the weight of my body drops down, mud coming out from under me and moving up over the sides of my body. I'm completely covered from my shoulders to my feet.

It takes all my effort to slowly roll myself out from under the heavy mass, and I lie there exhausted as the water washes over my body.

"You cheated." I poke my tongue out while giving him a nasty look.

He props himself on his side. "Hey, it's not my fault you can't control your powers better."

"Well, considering you seem to be the one in charge of teaching me, I'd say it's your fault. You just wait."

"For what?" He leans in closer.

My heart races faster and I swear he can see it. "For payback."

"I don't think there's a bone in your body that could hurt someone." He reaches over and places a wet strand of hair behind my ear.

My breathing is quick and shallow. To make matters worse, I do the one thing that I shouldn't and meet his gazing eyes.

"What about you?" I ask.

"What about me?"

"Does the negative influence in you make you a bad person?"

He stares at me a moment longer and softly replies, "No," before his hand slides under my neck, lifting my chin. His soft lips reach mine not a second after and the feeling is electrifying. I let out a sigh and press back into him, intensifying the kiss.

My whole world has been turned upside down the last few days, but there's nothing about this moment that feels anything but right. His hand grabs my bare waist, the sudden change in pace startling me. It takes all my effort to push him away. I'm expecting him to be disappointed, but he has the same perplexed look as yesterday.

He chuckles and I'm not sure how to respond.

"I'm sorry–" I begin.

"Don't," he says firmly, shaking his head. "Don't ever apologize for behaving the way you want. You have no idea how nice it is to finally know that someone is responding to me exactly the way they want to, not because they're possibly being influenced to. Don't get me wrong, I hate it when you push me away, but it's nice to know that that's exactly what you're feeling in that moment." He stares deep into my eyes, as if he's desperate for me to hear him. "It's hard knowing how our influence is affecting other people. I've dated girls who've continued to date me, not because they liked me, but because it fulfilled some negative thought they were trying to satisfy. Like pissing off their parents, or maybe using me to try and make another guy jealous."

He runs his hands through his hair and walks away.

Now he can't see me, I press my fingers to my lips and close my eyes. Why did I push him away? I've always moved around so I've never felt the need to build a relationship as it was only destined to end. Plus, I would have never been allowed out on a date. I can tell by the way he moves around me that intimacy isn't new to him, as it is to me. It needs to be a conversation we have soon because continuing to push him away for moving too fast is only going to make him think I'm not interested, which is definitely not the case.

I can't deny, though, that everything about what has happened seems as if it has played out perfectly. There's something about him that I've been drawn to ever since I met him, and I think he feels it too.

His last statement sends a pang of sadness through me. Will this influence we have always make me question the intentions of people around me? Are they acting that way because of who they are, or because they're reacting to me? I let out a long sigh. Today has been more complex than I could have imagined.

Vincent comes back over and hands me a spare towel and I can sense that this is the end of our afternoon out here.

"Just because I emit a negative energy, that doesn't make me a bad person," he says softly, staring at me with intensity.

"I'm sorry I insinuated you were a bad person. You've been nothing but kind to me since we met, and I can't thank you enough."

My heart races as I step closer and intentionally take his hand for the first time. There's so much uncertainty around me with everything that I've learned, but this right here– Vincent and me–I'm nothing but sure about.

CHAPTER ELEVEN

For the first time I wake feeling refreshed and can tell it's nowhere near time to leave. I take the opportunity to get in some element training and manage to hold my whirlwind for fifty-two seconds before my reserves run low. That's over three times longer than yesterday. I quickly regenerate and attempt my first ever second whirlwind in a row. The strength and speed are lacking in comparison to the first, but I manage to hold out for thirty-two seconds before my head starts spinning.

I release my hold and lie back, panting as I recover. There doesn't feel to be enough time in the day, so I'll be glad to see the end of school this week. I could achieve so much more if I had the whole day to train. I've never felt so determined about anything in my life. Learning to control my gift is my complete and utter focus.

Well, almost my complete focus. I hear a car arriving and look up to see Vincent emerging from his pickup. He raises his eyebrows when he sees me lying on the grass, but I just smile and wave to reassure him I'm fine. Training this morning has taken less than five minutes, but I'm utterly exhausted. Considering that's how I've felt at the end of every training session so far, but that I've accomplished so much more today, I can take some reassurance that I'm slowly getting better.

By the time we make it inside, the fresh smell of toast wafts through the living room and my stomach groans.

Pop emerges from the kitchen with a smile that reaches his weary eyes.

"Breakfast will be done by the time you finish getting ready. If you're hungry, that is."

I give him a genuine caring smile in return. "That'd be lovely, thanks."

I quickly get ready for school, then join Pop and Vincent for breakfast. Aunt Amy has usually left for work by the time I get up for school so I either eat on my own, or with Lily on the odd occasion, so today's breakfast feels somewhat sentimental.

My thoughts remind me of a question I've been meaning to ask since yesterday. "So, am I actually related to Lily and Aunt Amy? Given Lily is a fire wielder she stems from a different family line to me, doesn't she?"

Pop and Vincent exchange glances, but it's Pop who responds. "Family doesn't always mean blood relation. They've been a part of your life more than most relatives."

I nod in response and quickly finish my breakfast. His response makes me question why I'd even asked. Did it even really matter? Aunt Amy basically raised me since my mom left to fight XET, and Lily has been more like a sister than anything. An annoying, extremely frustrating big sister.

Vincent and I make our way to the drop off point, and I take the lead driving again, this time without errors. I remind him that I'll be late this afternoon, but he surprises me by saying he won't be waiting anyway. Apparently, he has work commitments. I must admit I feel a twinge of sadness knowing he won't be there this afternoon.

The school day goes by uneventfully. I pass Lily several times, but she refuses to make eye contact. Well, two can play at that game!

After school, I quickly make my way to Walmart to buy a phone. I head straight to the phone section and attempt to sort out what I need. Essentially, I just want something simple for calling people in an emergency, or texting. I readily accept the offer for help from the store clerk. She picks out a phone and a month-to-month prepaid SIM, and even goes through the process of setting it up. I thank her and pay for the phone using a debit card Aunt Amy gave me for emergency situations. Technically this isn't an emergency, but if I ever needed to be contactable in an emergency, then I'll need a phone. I'm sure she'll understand.

I quickly glance around the rest of the store and decide to go for a walk through. It's such a different experience when you have all the time in the world to just wander around. Usually, I'm following Aunt Amy up and down the aisles.

I decide to start with the grocery section. As much as I appreciate Pop's hospitality, there are certain treats I'm dying for. As I walk past an aisle, a slight movement catches my eye. I slow my pace to quickly reassess what I think I saw. Two women are down an aisle alone and I could swear I saw one place something in her bag. My heart races. *What do I do?*

Before jumping to conclusions, I decide to move closer to try and hear what they're saying. I make my way down a parallel aisle and listen through the merchandise. They're talking in hushed voices, so I can't pick out anything clearly. Something in the pit of my stomach makes me feel that what I saw was correct. They're pocketing store items.

My first instinct is to find a store representative and tell them, but a thought pops in my head which intrigues me. What if I could influence them positively to put the items back? By now I've been nowhere near Lily for an hour, but I'm not sure if that is long enough. How close will I need to stand to them? And how long will I need to stand by them?

I decide I have nothing to lose and for the next half an hour I stay close to the two women, but always staying in the aisle over. I keep holding out hope that I'll hear them admit to each other that what they're doing is wrong, and put the items back, but that never happens. I finally attempt one last strategy and head down the aisle they're in. Maybe if I'm right by them I'll have a stronger influence?

As soon as I walk into the aisle, they turn their backs to me and step closer to one another. I take a moment to look them over. Their clothes are worn and faded, and judging by the state of their hair, they're in need of a decent haircut.

Once I'm close enough, I turn away from them, focusing on the selection of sweets in front of me. When I had turned into the aisle one of the women was holding a chocolate bar and hasn't made a move to put it back.

"Lucy's been asking for months to try this new flavor," one woman says in a solemn voice.

"You know we can't get caught up on indulgences," the other woman chastises, and walks away.

I pick up a packet in front of me and blankly stare at it, not even taking in the color or writing before I put it back. I take a couple of steps closer to the remaining woman who hasn't moved. *Please just put it back!*

The candy wrapper rustles, as if she's turning it over and over in her hands, followed by the unmistakable sound of her bag opening.

I couldn't do it.

My head drops and I find myself holding back tears as I quickly walk away. My haste seems to catch the attention of the store clerk who served me earlier.

"Are you okay, hon?"

I hesitate. As I start to speak, I notice something in the distance above her head. Security cameras.

"No, I'm fine thanks." The tension in my shoulders relax. I leave the ladies in the hands of the store and hope their security measures are enough to catch them.

———

It's late afternoon by the time I get home, and Pop's waiting for me inside, dinner already cooked. Vincent had said a few days ago that Pop doesn't usually eat this much but he seems eager to cook and I must make more of an effort to tell him how much I appreciate it. He always greets me with the biggest, warmest hugs and his mood is contagious.

"I've got to head out tonight so will need the Jeep. I'll have it back by morning," he informs me once we've finished eating.

I remember Vincent saying that Pop rarely leaves the cabin. So much so that Vincent has to do his groceries. I feel uneasy questioning him, but I sense he's hiding something.

"Sure, it's your Jeep, so you don't need to ask permission." I shift awkwardly as I formulate a lie. "Vincent said he won't be here tonight and I'm not quite comfortable being on my own; any chance I can come with you?"

Pop looks me up and down. I wonder if he can see through the lie. "I'm sorry, Kaylee, but you can't come."

He's not trying to lie to me but he's not explaining anything either.

"Where are you going?" I'm starting to realize that I'm not

getting anywhere in life by dancing around what I want to say.

He clears his throat and stares at me a second longer. "Maria has asked me to follow up on some activity from XET in Charlotte. She managed to put a tracker on their vehicle but there's been no movement since the weekend, and she has asked if I could see if they've dumped the vehicle or if they're still there."

My stomach drops. "Please don't leave me here alone. I won't get in your way. I'll hide on the backseat. Whatever you ask." Now I'm not lying.

His face softens. "Kaylee–"

"Please, Pop," I beg. "You said there's a possibility they're not even there."

He hesitates, then sighs. "You do exactly as I say, when I say it."

I should be happy he's not leaving me on my own, but that means I'm about to head toward the enemy. I quickly nod in response and get in the vehicle before he changes his mind.

Now that we have time to talk, I finally ask the question that's been nagging at me since the incident in Walmart.

"Pop, today I saw two women shoplifting, and I followed them around to try and use my positive influence to make them stop. But it didn't work."

He shakes his head with a look of bewilderment. "Only you would try and influence someone into making the better choice. Just because you influence someone positively, it doesn't mean the action they undertake is going to seem positive to you."

"I don't understand."

"We can't pretend to imagine what these women are going through, but it's likely that your influence was working. Let's say they come from poverty. While stealing isn't generally seen as a positive action, it can be if the food is preventing them from starving. The positive result comes from having a fed, contented family. Whereas someone else who doesn't have such a powerful motivation for stealing, for example a teenager who just wants the latest fashion accessory, would be influenced by you not to steal as fulfilling greed isn't a positive action."

I take a moment to mull that over. My influence doesn't necessarily mean they'll act in a way that I perceive as positive.

Pop continues, "Every person, every day, has their own personal struggles going on in their mind. They all have their own moral compass and that will determine if each action they take is positive or negative. Take something as simple as exercising more. For the general population, if they were around a positive influence, it would heighten that voice in their head to the point that they would probably go for a walk or undertake some sort of exercise. However, if a professional dancer was around the positive influence and up until that point she had been training herself to exhaustion, while she might be thinking *I need to train more*, deep down she knows that doing so could put her body at risk of injury. Being around the positive influence would make her take that much-needed rest."

I sigh. "So, we really don't have any control of our influence, because even if we tried to use it, the response could be the complete opposite?" I don't think there's any hope of controlling this part of me.

"It really depends on the context. Vincent uses his influence at his parties to increase the alcohol intake, and therefore makes a bigger profit margin. In those circumstances, people are going to these parties with the intention to drink, so the negative influence basically has the same response to everyone there, that is to drink a little more."

I stare at Pop in shock. Vincent's purposely making people drink more just so he can make money. The thought leaves a sour taste in my mouth. Is that why he shares his energy? So people are more awake to stay out longer and therefore buy more alcohol?

Pop seems to catch on to my feelings. "Does Vincent seem like the sort of person who's using the money he makes for fancy clothes or cars?"

"No," I admit. Vincent is always dressed tidily, but he doesn't have an expensive watch or car, or anything more than the necessities.

"I can't work, and your mother doesn't make an income either," Pop adds on, pausing as if to wait for me to connect the dots. "I don't have an expensive lifestyle out here, but I do go through some groceries, clothes, and supplies. Vincent covers those expenses for me, just as Amy covers those expenses for you and Lily. And whatever money is left over is put aside to go toward the next relocation, which happens a lot and is more expensive than you realize. Any extra income goes to funding your mom and the others at Headquarters. Can you blame Vincent for taking advantage of his abilities to try and make life a little easier? He's only nineteen, but has been working to support Tyler, himself and me for a few years now."

I'd been meaning to have a conversation with Vincent about his work. It hadn't sat well with me since I found out about his job, but now, realizing what he's supporting, it's hard to be judgmental.

"Why do you live alone?" I thought we were supposed to live in pairs.

"When Tom was killed by XET–"

"Wait. Uncle Tom? Lily's father? I thought he died during a home invas..." I take a sharp inhale and a nauseating sensation courses through my stomach. XET killed Uncle Tom. I was too young at the time to remember that night.

"Yes, Lily's father. XET had found where you were living. Tom kept them distracted while you all escaped. His death–and knowing how close XET had come to you and Lily–was the driving force behind your mother going to join the fight against them. At that time, I was paired with Janice–your grandmother–but she went with Maria too. I'd always lived an isolated lifestyle, and your mother asked if I would stay with your family as extra protection for you and Lily should the need arise. When your mother comes home, we pair up to reduce her influence, but when she's away, I happily keep to myself."

So much pain has been caused by XET. But surely killing them isn't our only option, otherwise where does the suffering end?

A couple of words stand out from what Pop just said. "How come you like being by yourself?"

Maybe he wishes I wasn't staying with him?

"I..." He clears his throat. "I became addicted to stealing energy. It's just easier to avoid the temptation if I distance myself from people."

My conversation with Vincent rings in my mind.

Have you killed anyone?

No. Although I know people who have.

"I'm sorry, I didn't mean to pry."

"You've got nothing to apologize for, child, my demons are my own to bear."

"Would you prefer if I didn't stay at the cabin?" I ask, genuinely concerned me being there isn't good for him.

"Goodness, no. It's actually nice having some company

again." He turns to me and gives me a smile, which I reciprocate.

It takes just under three hours to get to Charlotte and finally Pop's driving begins to slow down. The big blue and red sign of Motel 6 stands out as we make our way closer. My heart thumps harder as he slowly pulls into the driveway next door and parks at the back of Wendy's parking lot.

"Listen very carefully," he says firmly. "I'm going next door to look for the car and scope out where they're staying. If you hear anything amiss, you drive away immediately. And if I'm not back within ten minutes you drive away immediately. Do you understand?"

I slowly nod; my mouth suddenly too dry to talk.

"This could be my only chance to catch them by surprise and I don't want to be worrying about your safety. Do not leave the car," he reinforces.

What does he mean *catch them by surprise*? I thought this trip was purely to see if they're here or not?

"Pop..." I call, but he's already shut the door behind him.

I climb over to the driver's seat, ready to act should the need arise. I stare at the solid white fence in front of me, the only thing preventing me from seeing Pop. My hearing is intensified as I try and listen for anything that might suggest something has gone wrong. Each second feels like an eternity as I continue to stare ahead, almost willing the fence to go invisible so I can see what's happening.

I'm focused so intensely that I scream as someone tries to open the driver's door. My heart is in my throat and a wave of nausea courses through me.

I'm so startled that I can't seem to move, despite looking into familiar blue eyes. Pop places his palm against the door and the door unlocks.

I look up at him, startled again. *But I have the keys!*

I climb back over to the passenger seat as I ask, "How did you do that?"

He holds up his hands. "Metal is an earth element."

I haven't seen Vincent manipulate metal. Perhaps there are different components that each can control?

Pop quickly gets in the Jeep and we drive away.

"What happened?" I ask. He couldn't have even been gone five minutes.

"The car was in the lot but building a layer of dust. I figured they'd dumped the car. I stood outside their hotel door for a minute but couldn't hear anything so took my chances to peek inside."

Having just seen how he got in the car, there's no question how he got in the hotel.

"The place didn't look as if it'd been touched at all, except for this sitting on the bed."

He holds up a small device in his hands.

I take it from him and turn it over.

"The car tracker," Pop clarifies.

A lump forms in my throat as I look around outside. "Are they watching us?"

"I don't think so. I think it was a message to say that they're smarter than we are. They want us to know they're out there and we can't stop them."

I really hope he's right about them not following us. Regardless, I regenerate and keep my eyes focused while we drive home.

I'm not sure at what point I fell asleep, but a firm hand shakes my shoulders.

"Kaylee," Pop says, firmer than I'd expect.

I quickly sit to attention. "What's going on?"

"It could be nothing, but I need you to climb over and take the wheel."

What? I look around us and we're back within the national park, just under half an hour away from the cabin. As I turn around, I notice a car following closely. My heart races and Pop says my name to regain my focus.

I awkwardly climb over onto the driver's seat as Pop moves out of the way. I grab the steering wheel with shaking hands, trying to keep the Jeep traveling straight as I sit down. I accelerate back up to the speed limit once I'm in control.

"Not far up ahead there's a right turn that I want you to take, okay?"

I nod, too nervous to talk. In the dead of the night, the forest gives off an eerie feeling which doesn't help right now.

The turnoff is looming and at Pop's instructions I turn off the high beams and quickly brake and take the turn. I continue along the road, constantly checking the rearview mirror for signs of the other car. About twenty seconds pass before the unmistakable shine of headlights flashes in the mirror.

My breathing accelerates. Has XET followed us from the hotel?

"I need you to speed up, Kaylee, and when I tell you, turn hard right into the forest."

"What?" It almost comes out like a squeal. Drive into the forest?

"You said when you wanted to come along that you would do whatever I said. This is that moment."

I nod slightly, gripping the steering wheel firmly as my hands sweat, and press my foot harder on the accelerator.

Pop looks out the window to the right. "Not yet... Not yet... Now!"

I brake as I turn the wheel to the right, the wheels screeching, and the headlight now shining straight into... rows of trees!

Pop throws his hands in front of him and I scream as the trees tear from the ground and move to the side, leaving just enough space to squeeze the vehicle through. The Jeep bounces and crunches as we travel along the uneven ground of holes and roots. Pop commands me to stop and turn off the engine. I slam against the brakes and turn the key. Darkness swallows us. At the same time the earth shakes behind me and as I stare into the rearview mirror, I can just make out the trees setting back into the ground they'd been ripped from, enclosing us in the forest.

My breathing is ragged as I stare into the mirror, waiting for any signs of lights pointing toward where we are. Seconds pass, then minutes, but there's no signs of anyone else. A warm hand lays on my shoulder, causing me to jump as Pop says my name.

My hands still clench tightly against the steering wheel, refusing to budge.

"We're okay," Pop says.

I nod my head slowly, repetitively.

"I need you to turn the engine back on, Kaylee. I can't get us out of here and drive at the same time."

I take another couple of moments to calm my racing mind, then command my body to move. With shaking hands, I turn the engine back on and set the vehicle in reverse. Much more slowly this time, I drive through the forest back to the road as Pop creates a path. Once we're back on the road, I stop, and Pop comes over to the driver's side. He lifts me out of the vehicle—my body still in too much shock—and places me in the passenger seat.

"I'm sorry, Kaylee. I don't think it was XET, but I wasn't about to take the risk."

"I'm okay," is all I can manage to say. I repeat it again in my head, hoping this time I'll believe it.

I remain on high alert until the cabin comes into view and finally some of the tension resolves. Pop gives me a big warm hug as we exit the Jeep. I let myself melt into the safety of his arms and my exhaustion slams into me.

It's close to midnight, so I make my way to the quiet of my—well, Vincent's—bedroom. I snuggle myself into his blankets. My mind remains insistent on replaying tonight's scare, so I try and divert my thoughts to Vincent. As I think about him, my mood lifts and I realize how much I miss him. I hope he'll be back tomorrow. For a short while, the distraction works but needless to say, it becomes another restless night.

CHAPTER TWELVE

Pop is waiting for me when I wake in the morning. We don't speak about last night, but I can tell he's trying to be a presence if I need to talk. Right now, I'm not sure what I need to do. I'd never been so scared in my life. Even if it wasn't XET following us, it solidified their threat to our kind, to me.

School passes in a blur, my mind too numb to focus on the exams. If Lily was there, I never noticed.

By the time I make it back to the cabin, I realize I've lost a day thinking about the threat of XET. I know I can't train at school, but I can use the time to strengthen my connection to air, and to speed my ability to regenerate. Yet today, I did nothing. I need to snap out of it, otherwise XET wins. The anxiety I'm harnessing from last night is only serving to distract me when now more than ever I need to focus on training.

Vincent wasn't here when I returned to the cabin, either. I don't have his number yet to see when he'll be returning. My mood drops again.

He's been so patient with me with regards to training and

our developing bond. He's officially my first kiss. And second and third. The thought causes a blush to warm my cheeks.

Again, Vincent comes to the aid of settling my mind. With clarity in thought, I focus on my whirlwind, which is now more like a mini tornado.

Suddenly, a movement on the outside of the dusty tornado captures my attention and the wind falls into dead silence. The young man begins clapping and walks toward me. The hair on the back of my neck stands to attention as I stare unmoving at the unfamiliar face. At approximately six-foot-tall and robust, I wouldn't be any match for him.

"Ah, the reclusive positive air." He steps closer.

I have no idea how to react. Do I put my hands up in defense? Do I run away? Do I scream? After last night's scare, my body shuts down. Frozen.

He reaches his hand toward me and I finally choose to run, but before I take a step he says, "Hi, I'm Tyler," offering me his outstretched hand.

Deep brown eyes stare at me. They are just a shade lighter than his skin tone. He has styled short black hair, with a trimmed goatee that outlines his voluminous lips. When I look closer, his body shape and his stance are familiar. Vincent. They may only be half-brothers but there are definite similarities. He's giving me a friendly smile with perfectly aligned teeth.

I reach for his outstretched hand. "Kaylee... I'm Kaylee." I let out a sigh of relief as my adrenaline subsides. *Anything! You could have done anything, yet you stood still?* As our hands connect, the warmth from his hand radiates up my arm, sending a calming sensation throughout my body. I don't know if it's because he reminds me of Vincent but I'm completely at ease around him. I finally smile back.

"That was pretty cool what you did back there," he says.

"Thanks. I'm going through one of those *my whole life is a lie and I have powers* moments in my life. You know, the usual."

He chuckles. "Well you seem to be getting a good grasp on it all."

"Thanks. What are you doing here, anyway?"

"Pop asked for some more groceries. Vincent wasn't sure when he was coming back out so figured I'd offer."

A heartfelt smile emerges as I help Tyler put the groceries away. More food for dinners by the looks of it. Pop said he enjoyed having me here and maybe he meant it.

"Is Pop around?" he inquires.

"He was gone by the time I returned from school, so I don't actually know where he is."

"Damn. He's probably gone hunting. Do you mind if I hang around and wait a little longer?"

"Technically, I'm the stranger here so you don't need my permission." I feel a sense of duty to keep him entertained but want to make use of all my available time. "I don't mean to be rude, but I really should get back to training."

"Do you want a hand?" he asks eagerly.

"That'd be amazing," I reply with a smile, and I'm suddenly pleased he's staying.

I catch him up to date on what I know and my progress so far. I must admit, it's odd saying what I'm doing out loud. It's basically solidifying that this really is my life now.

"The whirlwind is the first thing I've been able to achieve with air, but ultimately I'd like to learn to control it to defend or attack."

He gives me a smug look.

"Create a whirlwind for me."

I'd already regenerated on our way outside so was ready to go. I catch the next thread of wind and spiral it from my feet to my head. Tyler places his hand palm down in front of him and to my amazement small droplets of water rise to make a ball under his palm. Suddenly, the ball is hurled toward me and I jump in shock as it shatters like a water balloon right in front of my face. My whirlwind falls but I'm completely dry.

Tyler walks over to me, smiling. "Your whirlwind is already a defense mechanism. You can use it like a barrier to protect you from an incoming attack—say a water ball for example."

I'd never really thought about the fact the whirlwind was encasing me like a shelter. I wonder how strong I can make it.

"I have an idea," I state. "I want to create another whirlwind to see if a stronger attack can get through."

Tyler gives me a mischievous grin and we both ready ourselves.

I recreate my whirlwind, continuing to feed threads of wind into the base to build strength. I focus on maintaining a steady pace and once I'm confident it's stable, I nod again to Tyler. A ball forms in his hand—much larger than last time—and then he throws it directly at me. Everything moves in slow motion as it heads toward me. When it hits my barrier, it bursts and sprays off to the left, as the force of my counter-clockwise barrier drifts it off-center.

I literally jump with joy. He raises his eyebrows as he creates another ball, but this time it rotates, building speed. I plant my feet firmly on the ground and raise my arms, picking up the barrier, welcoming the challenge. As soon as I nod, the ball is heading in my direction. In any other circumstance I would have had no chance to block it. I couldn't even follow it with my eyes. It hits the barrier at top speed and shatters, water spraying to the left again.

But I'm not finished yet. I'm feeling devious and want to

try something else. I shout out, "Attack!" hoping he'll understand. Any other words and I'll lose concentration. Tyler seems to nod in understanding. I raise my arms and focus on gaining control of the top of the whirlwind. Once I have a firm grasp, I rotate my arms once counterclockwise above my head, then throw them forward, hoping the threads will continue.

The threads of wind twine around each other, traveling forward like a javelin, which hits him square in the chest, knocking him off balance. My mood changes immediately from elation to worry.

I take a step toward him, but my knees give way as my body tries to scramble for any shred of energy left, and I sink to the ground. The weight of my eyelids triples and I struggle to keep my eyes open. Tyler's already back on his feet and he rushes to me. His gentle hands encase mine and a warmth radiates from his hands into me. I sense his energy, giving it a dark brown color to match his eyes. It flows throughout my body and I forcefully open my channels to accept the exchange.

After being so exhausted, the effects are more intensified. I sense the energy slowing and grasp firmly onto Tyler's hands, sensing he has more to offer. He tries to pull away, but I cling to him, hungry for more.

Every time I've regenerated, I've always felt fulfilled, but now all I can sense is the empty space that isn't occupied, calling out for more. It thrives on each thread that is being passed to me, but as Tyler's energy stops, a deep ache courses through my body and charges toward our connected hands, sensing there's more on the other side. The empty feeling inside me screams out and I can't stop myself from trying to fill that void.

I close my eyes to focus on breaking down his barrier. My

body rejoices the moment it breaks through and grabs on to his bounty. Now I have a hold of it, I'm aware of how much more there is available, and I want it. No, I need it.

I let out a groan of relief as it passes through to me, and I put every ounce of strength in my body behind my grasp on him as he forcefully tries to pry me off, but his strength dwindles as his energy is passed along. The intense void within me completely encompasses my senses as it draws my sole focus to his energy, the outside world diminishing. I expected the ache to settle but it just grows stronger and stronger the closer it is to being filled.

Suddenly our hands are pried apart as I'm yanked away from Tyler. I thrash around, trying to escape the hands that clutch my arms and a guttural growl erupts from my chest. The sound shocks me awake. Vincent has a hold of me, his face tense with fury.

I quickly remember Tyler and look to him on the ground, panting on his hands and knees.

"Tyler," I call out in a half sob. "I'm so sorry."

Vincent releases his hold on me, and I reach down to Tyler. He raises his hand to gesture that he's okay and gets to his feet. I don't know how to make it better. I'm so honestly sorry and embarrassed. The tears sting at the back of my eyes and I fight to keep them at bay. Vincent hasn't said a word. He just keeps staring at his brother.

"It was my fault. I should have been more careful," Tyler replies to me.

I'm lost for words. I can't believe he's trying to blame himself. I'm the one who lost control.

"You're absolutely right. This was your fault," Vincent says before I have a chance to speak. "You're lucky I was here because she could have killed you."

I go to rebut Vincent, but the last two words ring through

my mind. I could have *killed him.* I process the fact that I was literally trying to steal all his energy, and in that moment, I couldn't stop myself and Tyler wasn't able to stop me. I gasp. *I could have killed him!*

"Don't be so melodramatic, Vince." Tyler rolls his eyes.

"Melodramatic?" Vincent snorts. "Let's see how much energy you have left, then."

Suddenly a large ball of debris flies toward Tyler, followed by another, and another. Tyler throws up a large wall of thick water. I cover my mouth in shock. Tyler was obviously holding back on me. Ball after ball hits his shield and get suctioned into the water, breaking apart into thousands of pieces of dirt, tainting his clear barrier.

Tyler begins to sway but Vincent is relentless in his attack.

"Stop!" I cry out at Vincent as Tyler lowers to a knee, but Vincent ignores me and keeps attacking. "Vincent, stop!" I scream again and jump in front of him.

He stares at me with such anger in his eyes that I take a step back in fear. My reaction softens his face and his attack ceases. Tyler's wall crashes to the ground and he folds back down to his hands and knees.

"You should have known better," Vincent states to Tyler then walks off to the cabin.

The water has retracted back underground, and Tyler has flipped over onto his back, staring up into the sky.

"I'm really sorry." I need to make sure he understands my sincerity.

"I know, me too," he replies.

"You can have some back?" I lightheartedly chuckle, and I give him my hand to take back what belongs to him.

He laughs, but he doesn't take my hand. "Thanks, but I'll be good in a minute."

He lifts his shirt to wipe sweat from his face and I awkwardly try to avert my eyes to stop myself from staring at the definition across his torso. I'm intrigued by a dark purple circle on his stomach and I try and figure out what it is. It suddenly dawns on me that it's a bruise and I gasp, realizing that it was from me. Without thinking I reach down and touch it. Tyler stares at me touching his stomach and my face flushes. I retract my hand quickly and stumble for words.

"I... ah... sorry, it's just..."

He breaks out in laughter. "You're welcome to touch my stomach anytime you want."

My face flushes warmer and I know I must be bright red. This is humiliating. "Well, I was going to apologize for the bruise but now I'm not so sure."

He presses on the area and flinches. "Yep, that's going to be a good one."

As if I didn't already feel bad enough about the situation, now I have to add bruising him to the list.

"Give me a moment with him." He nods his head toward the cabin. "Wish me luck." He heads off to face his brother.

I can't hear anything smashing so that must be a good sign. Tyler finally emerges holding his keys.

"Did it go so badly that you're running away?" I ask cheekily to Tyler.

He smiles. "No, but I've got to head back anyway."

"What about seeing Pop?" I ask, not sure if he's forgotten why he stuck around.

"It's all good, another reason to return. Perhaps it'll give me a chance to help you with training again." He raises his eyebrows in question.

"Yeah, that'd be great. I feel bad making Vincent do all the work training me."

Tyler laughs. "Yes, because all he's had to say is how much he hates being isolated out here with you."

A blush forms at the thought of Vincent talking about me to his brother.

We say our goodbyes and when I turn around Vincent is waiting for me on the balcony.

CHAPTER THIRTEEN

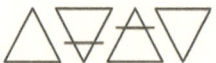

My hands start sweating as I make my way to Vincent. I haven't seen him in two days, and this is not how I wanted the reunion to go. I know I've let him down. I'm not sure how he's going to react to me. He warned me this could happen.

I take a deep breath and walk up the steps.

He rubs the back of his neck. I've come to notice that as a telltale sign that he has something on his mind, and it makes my stomach tie in knots.

"I had a chance to watch you and Tyler training for a little while. Your progress is astounding."

His compliment catches me off-guard and I wait for him to continue with a *but*. However, he just smiles. "Let's just forget about regeneration and training for the rest of the day and go for a swim?" he asks.

I look at him, confused, but considering the alternative is a discussion about what just happened, I happily oblige.

"Seriously though, no regenerating," he reinforces before we head off.

By the time we make it to the clearing, I basically sprint

toward the pool, ready for the cool water to wash off the sweat of this afternoon.

We end up sitting together in the shallow water catching up on the last two days. I'm not yet ready to talk about last night so I fill him in about my failed attempt at trying to stop someone from stealing which makes him laugh. Then I remember the second half of the conversation with Pop.

"Pop told me you use your influence to earn more money at work."

"It doesn't sound great when it's said out loud, but it is the truth. I'm good at my job, but that doesn't mean it's something I wish I was doing. We all play our own part whether it's fighting XET or funding our constant relocations."

I realize the pressure on his shoulders. Without parents–and a grandfather who is isolated–he and Tyler have had to take the brunt of the responsibility for finances. "How do you even find people that allow a nineteen-year-old to use their bar for an underage club or supply you with alcohol for the house parties?"

"You find those who are driven by money. It's a great motivator. When you add my influence to their already questionable character it doesn't take much convincing to get them to give me what I need."

It's hard to judge Vincent when my whole life I've been oblivious to the pressure and responsibilities that come with this life. I now understand that his motives for running the club are genuine. I think it's something that I need to accept is a part of him.

With the work topic over, the conversation flows easily, as if we've known each other a lifetime. A week ago, I could never have dreamed how much my life would change, and despite the threat of XET, it is all worth it for these moments here with Vincent.

Our eyes meet and Vincent reaches out for my hand but stops halfway.

My heart drops. The last two times we've been here I've pushed him away so maybe he thinks I'm not interested? Or maybe these two days apart have made him second guess his opinion of me? I figure I can't change the second option, but if he's hesitant because he thinks that I am, I can show him otherwise. This is my moment to show him I'm done pushing him away.

I shuffle closer toward him and press the side of my body against his. The warmth of his body along my arm and leg is a welcome sensation to the contrasting cool water around us. Electricity flows through my body where I'm pressed up against him, but this time something feels different. That deep guttural hunger awakens, realizing there's energy for the taking. I'm startled at the sudden urge to steal from him and do the one thing I vowed not to do again. I move away from him. I close my eyes and take some deep, frustrated breaths as I fight back tears. I can't bear to look at him. I know he's going to walk away again. Surely three times in a row is enough for him to be fed up with what seems like indecision.

"It's starting already, isn't it?" He breaks me out of my thoughts and when I open my eyes, he's still beside me. When I don't respond he follows with, "The stealing, Kaylee. Is that what you're feeling?"

I avoid making eye contact.

He reaches for my hand but stops himself again and makes a noise of frustration. Maybe he didn't touch me before because he was worried this would happen? He gets out of the water and walks off to grab his backpack.

"We need to go. Now!" he orders.

I hurry to follow him, not exactly sure what's happening.

"I thought we'd have more time than this, but you must

not have stolen as much as I thought." He checks to make sure I'm close behind him as he races down the trail. My breathing picks up as I struggle to keep up. "I told you the other day that stealing can be highly addictive, and the first time you fall from such a high can be the hardest to overcome. It can take a couple days for the hunger to finally settle, but I will be here for you, okay?"

The tension builds in my stomach. He's making this sound so serious. I'm fine. Surely, he's just being over dramatic?

We finally make it back to the cabin and I'm dripping with sweat again. My legs are aching from all the walking these last few days.

Vincent opens a door halfway along the hallway that I've never paid attention to before. Just inside the door is a shelf on the wall and he grabs down a lantern and some keys. He turns the lantern on which throws out a bright white light, and he motions for me to follow him. Stairs made from large flat rocks lead the way down, and as we descend, the wooden walls are replaced by rock walls.

As I reach the bottom of the steps I gasp.

Four cells aligned side-by-side in a ring—only disrupted by the staircase—stand before me. Thick bars cover the entrances with only the essentials inside; a bed and a hole in the ground I'm presuming to be a toilet.

I gape at Vincent, horrified.

"Vincent, what is this place? And why are we down here?" I take a step back onto the bottom stair.

"We hope we never need the cells, but if we ever capture someone from XET we need a secure place to hold them captive." He doesn't even seem fazed about what he just said. No trying to hide the fact that this world we live in isn't perfect. "For tonight, I'd like you to stay down here." He gives me a sympathetic look which causes me to laugh. He can't be serious?

"Okay, now I'm sure you're overreacting," I retort.

"Before you say no, will you do one thing for me?"

I roll my eyes but nod, waiting for his request.

"Go into one of the cells and regenerate."

I glance around the room again and shiver. Vincent's pleading eyes finally break my resolve and I give him a final *I'm doing this for you* look, and head into one of the cells. The bars screech as they slide along their unused tracks, which makes me cringe.

He locks me inside and I stare directly at him while I regenerate. I want to make sure he's looking right at me so once I'm done, he can see this is going too far.

The energy filters into my body, and I experience the usual heightened sensations. The feeling is so enlightening it even makes this dungeon seem tolerable. The pace begins to slow as I reach my regeneration limit, and I almost smile at Vincent to prove my point, but then a burning sensation pulls from deep within my stomach, screaming out for more.

What previously felt like a full, bursting absorption of energy, now feels meek and pathetic. My body can detect that regenerating hasn't filled me and it's furious.

I close my eyes and concentrate on regenerating again, but nothing shifts. My breathing accelerates as the hunger inside me churns. My head is screaming at me for more which makes it difficult to concentrate. I look around, and realization hits hard that I'm stuck in this cell with nothing but regeneration, and I almost let out a sob.

I look up at Vincent, about to beg for help, and then I get a sense of that deep blue energy that's just out of reach. The voice in my head goes into overdrive, begging me to find a solution, and I know who holds the key to my problem; both metaphorically and physically.

I plaster on the best smile that I can manage. My lips tremble and I dig deeper to try and control my movements.

"See, I told you there was nothing to worry about." My voice sounds foreign.

"I guess I was wrong," Vincent says calmly, with a shrug.

He moves closer to the door and the hunger in me intensifies, knowing I'm about to get what I desperately want. I edge my way slowly toward him, focused solely on his outstretched hand reaching for the door lock. I figure I'll have a couple of seconds to make my move while he's sliding the door open. I'll only have one chance, so I need to make it work.

He pauses for a brief second with his hand just out of reach.

"What you seem to forget, is that I've been where you are." He makes direct eye contact and retracts his hand as he takes a step back.

My mind goes frantic as my only chance of fulfillment steps away. I throw myself against the door and stretch my arm through the bars as far as possible but he's out of reach. This time I let out an audible cry as my hand misses him by mere inches. There's pain in his eyes as he watches me lose to the voice inside me, but I don't have the clarity to care.

The empty space inside me is like a deep black hole that is destined to remain unfulfilled. I've never craved something so badly and knowing that I can't do anything about it is distressing. The space around me caves in as I realize I'm trapped, and I react like any caught wild animal. I fight to escape.

I grab hold of the bars and shake them with as much force as I can manage. The door rattles in reply but remains tightly locked. I let out a yell of frustration and my body shakes as the pent-up anger is released. I'm not strong enough. Or am I?

I take a couple steps back to think, and Tyler's balls of water come to mind. I focus on the air in front of me and I begin to rotate it into a small sphere. The ball turns a light brown color as the debris from the room is pulled into it, which causes Vincent to hurry toward the stairs.

I stare at the door and focus my rage into the sphere as it gathers speed. When my legs begin to falter, I know my only chance is to release the ball now, or risk completely depleting myself. I plant my feet and thrust the ball of wind forward as forcefully as possible. The door clashes against its tracks and the room is filled with the screeching sound of metal grinding against metal.

The cloud of dust subsides, and I slowly walk over to the door. As I attempt to slide the door open it catches against the lock and won't move any farther. I pull again and again, harder and harder. Finally, my spirit breaks as I accept defeat. My hands drag down the bars, aching, and I slump onto the floor. I press my back against the cell wall and hug my knees to my chest and slowly rock back and forward. The pain of the rock digging into my back helps soothe the unfulfilled darkness in me and my mind gets lost in the rhythmic on-off pressure. The tears roll down my cheeks, leaving a cold wet path behind. No sound escapes.

Vincent slowly walks over and sits on the opposite side of the door. I can't bear to look at him. I'm ashamed of my reaction, but there was nothing I could do to control myself.

"Please just make it go away," I beg him.

"I can't," he replies. "This is something that you need to learn to overcome on your own. But I will promise that it gets easier. The best thing to do for now is not to regenerate. As with any addiction, sometimes it's easier just to go cold turkey. Eventually we'll train you to regenerate without that overwhelming need to steal. Okay?"

"Okay," I reply softly. I've only had alcohol that one night, and never taken drugs, so I've never known what it's like to have an addiction. This overwhelming need to want something that you can't have is all-encompassing and it's hard to focus on anything else. "Tell me about your childhood," I ask Vincent, hoping for a distraction.

He gets up and walks into the cell beside me then emerges with a blanket.

"Put this on." He places the blanket on the floor close to the bars. I wrap it around me and shiver. I hadn't noticed how cold and tense I had become.

He sits down again and begins his story. "We had a good life growing up. I imagine the first few years were fairly similar to an ordinary upbringing apart from moving around frequently. My biological mother–who Tyler and I called Mom–home-schooled us until we were about nine, while Tyler's biological mother, Momma, worked. We knew about our gifts our whole life, and I imagine that was why we were home-schooled as we were too young to understand the risks of exposing us. Once we had a grasp on using our element and could understand that it needed to be kept secret, we were enrolled into mainstream schooling.

"I wasn't the most academically minded, so I put my focus into sports, whereas Tyler was the complete opposite. We basically grew up like twins as we're only a few weeks apart, so we always got along despite our differences."

Their relationship reminds me of the early years between Lily and me.

"That was until our teenage years. I'll be the first to admit that I had a short fuse during those years which made for some trying times, but I swear Tyler would purposely push my buttons.

"Growing up, we'd always had people whispering behind our backs about our family dynamic. I was fifteen when I was playing in a football game and the opposite team thought it'd be fun to make jokes about our moms. I used my abilities to trip them up during the game, so they had a humiliating defeat and scored a few bruises hitting the ground. Our moms saw what I'd done and pulled me out of school immediately. I refused to go back to home-schooling, so I got a job as an apprentice mechanic which kept my hands and head occupied. It was only a year later that our moms died. That night will be embedded in my memory forever."

He pauses and continues to stare at the ground.

"You don't have to talk about it if you don't want to," I reassure him.

"No, it's fine. It's just something that I don't talk about very often. So, it had been about three years since the last attack from XET and we had grown a false sense of security. We'd been living in Dallas for over two years, which was a record. We were having such a great day when Mom received a call from Maria saying they'd tracked XET to Dallas.

"We didn't want to take any chances so we packed as much as we could into our two cars and left. We had driven half the night and eventually had to stop to get gas. Everything seemed fine, but when we took off there was a car following us. I was in the car with Mom and we were trailing behind Momma and Tyler. We slowed down to allow the car to pass us, but once they were in front of Momma they slammed on their brakes. Momma didn't have enough time to stop and she ended up slamming into the back of their car. The moment we saw the men emerge from the car wielding guns we knew it was XET."

I unconsciously let out a gasp. It's no wonder Pop was so worried about the car trailing us last night. That's how XET attacked his daughter.

"I can remember Mom screaming at me to get Tyler. She threw up a shield, which let me get to the passenger seat. Tyler must have knocked his head as there was blood seeping down the side of his face, and he was hardly conscious. I basically had to carry him out of the car into our other car.

The sound of bullets raining down on Mom's shield penetrated the dark night. I went back to grab Momma, but Mom was shouting at me to get back in the car and leave. I'll never forget that pleading look in her eyes as she begged me to go. I don't know why I obeyed her. I'd known for years about XET and had put a lot of training into defending us, but I was so scared." His voice catches when he says *scared* and my heart breaks for him.

What I went through last night was only a fraction of what Vincent experienced and that was enough to shake me up quite a bit. I really wish I wasn't locked in the cage, because right now all I want to do is wrap my arms around him.

"Mom's shield was starting to crumble and she told me one last time to go and that she'd be right behind us. I don't think I'll ever forgive myself for turning my back on them that night and driving away. I drove back to the gas station and waited. The minutes felt like hours, but when they never arrived, I decided to go back. The sun was starting to rise, and I could see the vague outline of Momma's car in the distance. When we finally reached the car there was blood spattered on the road around it.

"Up until that point I think we'd held up some sort of hope that they had gotten away, but that was when we knew that they were gone. Tyler broke down and I knew I had to hold us together. I collected our bags from the smashed car, and then disposed of the car by sinking it into the ground. Apart from fuel I didn't stop driving until we reached Pop in San Francisco."

Silence overtakes us. I'm not sure how to respond. "I'm so very sorry, Vincent." It doesn't feel like enough.

He nods gently. "We stayed with Pop for just over a year so Tyler could graduate high school. Since then, we've traveled around a fair bit, not because of XET but because we had the freedom to do so. Every couple of months we come back and check in on Pop for a couple of weeks then head off again."

"Why don't you just stay with Pop?" I ask, more hopeful than I anticipated.

"To be honest, it isn't the best thing for a lot of us to be living together in the one area. They were okay with us staying for the year given we were still young, but now they prefer us to limit our time to no longer than a couple of weeks, two or three times a year. There's too many lives at risk with us in the one place."

It suddenly dawns on me that the heavy gnawing sensation in my stomach has settled down and my eyelids weigh heavily. I let the feeling take over, knowing this may be my only opportunity to rest without that deep guttural urge.

"I'll be upstairs, so call out if you need me," Vincent tells me as he gets up off the floor. "Just promise me you won't regenerate?"

"I don't want to regenerate ever again if that's how it makes me feel," I reply honestly.

He smiles sympathetically and leaves me in the cellar.

I lie down on the bed and attempt to get in a comfortable position on what feels to be a rock mattress, but surprisingly, rest comes easily.

CHAPTER FOURTEEN

I wake to the sound of footsteps, but also to darkness. My breath quickens as I try and figure out where I am as a white light filters through the room. As my eyes adjust, Vincent is on the other side of the cell door holding the lantern.

"What time is it?" I ask groggily.

"Almost eight o'clock."

"Crap, I've got to get ready for school!"

His eyebrows furrow. "Are you sure you don't want the day off?"

It takes a moment for me to register why, but I don't feel the hunger or pain for stealing. "I'm actually feeling okay, and I promised Mom that I'd go. Plus, Lily will be there to keep an eye on me." I add the last bit in, but I haven't quite told Vincent that we're not on speaking terms yet. Nevertheless, I'm being honest about my feelings. Apart from a sore back, I don't feel any different from usual. No internal force is screaming at me to hurt everyone around me.

He sighs, unlocks the door, and I quickly get ready for school.

"I'll see you back here after school?" Vincent asks when I

meet him outside at the Jeep, and I happily nod back. "You'll need to put more gas in." He hands me some money and I stare at him blankly.

"You don't need to give me money. You've done more than enough." I grab hold of his hand to give him the money back and as soon as we make contact, I sense his energy on the other side. I inhale deeply as my mind wanders to the possibilities, but as I gaze into his deep blue eyes, a stronger sensation overwhelms me. A desire to prove myself and more importantly, to protect him. I go against everything screaming inside my body and let go of his hand.

Vincent gives me a cheeky grin. "Lucky you made the right decision, otherwise I was going to taser you."

I'd forgotten about his taser! After yesterday's episode, I guess I can't blame him.

———

I'VE ALWAYS BEEN A VISUAL LEARNER, SO WHEN IT CAME TO seeing the energy we harness as a colorful entity, the visualization came easily. But now as I look around at my classmates, all I can see is the burning bright energy inside each of them. My knees shake up and down as I gnaw on the back of my pencil, failing to take my mind off the one thing I can't have. A chunk of wood falls on the table and I stare at the blank exam it sits upon. Technically, I have a one-in-four chance of getting the questions right just by answering A for everything, but I figure my mind could do with some distraction and I delve into the exam as much as I can manage.

When the lunch bell rings, I make my escape as quickly as possible, trying to avoid the onslaught of students. Right now, a bump in the shoulder from someone passing by would be my undoing.

Lily finds me huddled at a corner table by myself. "How long since you stole?" Her face is smug but there seems to be some sincerity in her voice. Is it that obvious that I'm struggling?

"Yesterday," I reply.

"You shouldn't be here today!"

"I'm fine. Really. I just need to make sure I never touch another person again in my life." I come across as joking, but deep down I feel I'm never going to be able to tolerate physical contact ever again if I keep reacting the same way.

"Don't be stupid," Lily responds in her typical blunt style. "You just need more time."

She sits down and toys around with the food on her plate, avoiding direct eye contact. "The past few years I've resented you so much."

She's resented me? What could she possibly be resentful of?

Answering my unspoken question, Lily continues. "Everyone was doing everything they could to keep this life from you. I know if I could have a do-over I would have preferred not to find out, which is the only reason I've kept my mouth shut. The whole time you were constantly begging me to help persuade our moms to give you more freedom and I just wanted to scream at you to be grateful for the life you'd been given.

"Despite all that, I was constantly hoping that each day would be the day you found out and that you'd come to me to help you through it. But each night you'd go to bed clueless and it was a constant reminder of how alone I was.

"Then it happened. You finally found out what we are but the last person you wanted to talk to was me. You didn't even want to live in the same house."

She looks back down at the table and for the first time in

years her walls come down. It seems we've both been wanting our friendship to go back to how it was, but we were both stuck in a cycle of wishing we had the other's life. I was so mad when I found out she knew and had been keeping it a secret, but I never once considered how it had been affecting her life.

"I'm sorry," I say sincerely. "I was angry when I found out that you'd been hiding this secret from me. It made me feel like such an outsider to my whole family. I couldn't understand why no one trusted me to know, but after realizing the threat of XET I'm starting to understand why Mom made this choice, not that I think it was the right choice." It's something I've been thinking about since the close call the other night. It's going to take a while to trust my family, but I'm slowly starting to forgive them. Plus, the anger I'm holding against everyone isn't doing me good. It's just adding more hurt.

"I don't think either of us was supposed to find out," she replies, "but your mom was put in a situation where she had to expose herself. Do you remember that car accident your mom and I had at school about two years ago?"

I remember the day vividly. "Yeah, a student ran the light and hit you guys."

"Well, to anyone else it might have looked as if the driver turned the wheel at the last moment, but I saw your mom throw her hands forward. An enormous dent appeared in the side of his car as it turned away suddenly and sharply, and only then did it graze our front bumper, so I knew something unexplainable had happened.

"I remember staring at Aunt Maria in awe and asking, *What did you just do?* She tried brushing me off and stating that I must have hit my head, but then you came running toward us and I saw her eyes open in horror. I'm not proud of what I did next, but I wanted answers and I could tell she was desperate for you not to know. I told your mom that you'd be so excited to hear what I had to say about her, and she pleaded with me not to tell you. I agreed, in exchange for answers."

The accident is a sight I will never forget. Mom had come home early to surprise me, and Lily was home sick, well, hiding from the exam that day. I'd heard the screech first and once I'd cleared through the cluster of students, I saw that one of the cars was Aunt Amy's. My heart had dropped at the sight, but there was hardly any damage to their car. So little damage that we were able to drive home. On the other hand, the student in the other car ended up being transported away via ambulance and his car was a write-off.

"Once you had gone to bed that night, I sought out your mom. I was expecting her to try and lie her way out of it, but she'd informed my mom and they were both waiting for me. In one night, I found out everything: about our past, our powers, XET. Nothing was left unsaid. By the time they'd finished talking I was so upset! I remember being so lost and that the one person I wanted to talk to about it, was the one person I had to keep it all a secret from."

My heart drops for her. It took a few days for me to gather all the information. Well, I think I have it all now? I couldn't imagine finding everything out in one night at this age, especially at fifteen. It makes sense though. That was the same time our relationship fell apart. "That must have been really hard," I say.

She gives me a small nod. "I started withdrawing from everyone and became so upset at the smallest things. To make matters worse, my hormones were a mess, so I was just one big ball of anger. Your mom was never around long enough to teach me anything, and my mom didn't know how it all worked, so I did the one thing any teenager does when they aren't getting their way. I rebelled.

"I started skipping school and some nights I wouldn't even bother coming home. It was the first time I'd ever been separated from you for more than a day and I could finally see the effect of our influence. I was desperate to know more so I threatened to run away unless they gave me more.

"The next day, Mom took me over to meet Pop, but it was also when I first met Vincent and Tyler."

My interest piques at the mention of Vincent.

"By this point, the guys had been staying with Pop almost a year and were looking at moving out in a couple months. They both helped me out on the weekends, and I can remember for the first time in a long time I felt normal. Well, as normal as you can be when you have abilities.

"It was gut-wrenching when they moved away. I went back to feeling alone again and can remember growing so much resentment toward you. I used to hold on to the hope that in the next few months they would return, even though it meant working for Vincent."

"What exactly is it that you do for Vincent?" She wasn't dressed as bar staff the two times I've seen her at his parties.

"I'm there for the same reason as he is. To influence people to drink more. Those clubs are his baby. I'm shocked he hasn't bragged yet." There's a hint of distaste in her voice.

I'm not about to divulge that I've already had that conversation with Vincent and know more than she probably does about his thoughts on it. My stomach turns at the thought of my next question. Every time Lily has spoken about Vincent it hasn't been in the greatest light. Considering he helped her with her skills it seems odd that they don't get along. I swallow the lump in my throat. "Did something happen between the two of you?"

"Who? Vincent?" She laughs, but her knee bounces up and down under the table. "I may have been young and naïve when he was teaching me, but all it took was one night in the club to see him for what he is."

"What do you mean?"

She must notice the way I'm hanging off her every word. "Oh no, Kaylee. Please trust me when I tell you he's not good news. He'll use you the way he uses them all, then he'll move onto the next. I've seen it time and time again."

I look down at my hands, uncertain of how to reply. I don't know how to feel about what she's said. Vincent hasn't shown himself to be anywhere near the person she's describing so doesn't he deserve the opportunity to prove himself?

The lunch bell rings, but I'm not done with our conversation. I have so many more questions. Lily hurries to tidy up her lunch and I sigh as I realize we have another test.

"I'm sorry," I call out to Lily as she heads off in the opposite direction. She pauses and I clarify, "I'm sorry that I wasn't able to be there for you when you found out. It's going to take a while to work through my feelings from being lied to, but I honestly am trying."

She gives me a small smile, and then we both head off to our separate exams.

At the end of the school day, I decide to wait for Lily. Surely, we can start mending from here? I decide to begin that journey. "I'm meeting up with Vincent soon, but once this week is over you should come to Pop's and train with me."

"You know you can come home, right? I can help you out."

"I really appreciate that," I reply with as much sincerity as I can, "but out there I don't need to worry about other people seeing me and I have the space to practice without fear of breaking something."

Lily stares down at her feet. "Oh, okay, I guess I'll see you tomorrow then."

———

"Jump in, I want to take you somewhere," Vincent calls out to me once I reach the cabin.

I hop in the passenger seat of his pickup and get prepared for a long journey as usual, but this time we arrive in less than five minutes.

We walk for a short while and finally emerge on a ledge overlooking the forest. The terrain of the forest is so much more rugged than I imagined, and I stare out at the rolling hills in front of me. The sun slowly lowering off in the distance. There's only a small amount of space before the edge drops down the side of the cliff so I'm extra cautious with my footing.

Vincent lays a blanket on the ground and I take a seat. How could he ever be the person Lily thinks he is?

We sit together taking in the view in silence. The moment isn't awkward, as we're so entranced by the beauty of our surroundings.

"I figured that while you can't regenerate, you'd like something a bit quieter and away from people tempting you." He breaks the silence.

I stare at him in awe. I've never met anyone so thoughtful and kind. Instinctively I reach out to him but stop just short. I could almost cry.

"I know I said it yesterday, but you seem to fit seamlessly into our lifestyle. It hasn't taken you long at all to get through everything I've thrown at you." He reaches into his pocket.

"But just in case I'm wrong, I'll keep this close by." He pulls out the taser and places it beside him. He offers me his hand, but I hesitate.

I gaze deeply into his eyes and my body responds before my brain can over-think and I take hold of his hand.

After a few minutes, he pulls me down beside him and places his arm under my neck. Every inch of skin that is pressed up against him has come to life. I set up mental barriers along my body to try to give myself the opportunity to enjoy this moment rather than lying here obsessing about the proximity of the thing I want the most. I take a deep, calming breath to clear my mind and as I inhale, his earthy scent infiltrates me and sends a wave of longing through my body. If there was anything that could have taken my mind off the burning hunger inside of me, it's the deeper longing that I've been holding back toward Vincent.

Once I'm certain I'm in control, I roll to my side and rest my head on his chest. I listen to his heart beating underneath and he squeezes me tightly.

As the sun eventually fades from view and the night sky takes over, the lights of the city on the outskirts of the forest grow thicker until there's a sea of lights in the distance. The scene is completely breathtaking, and I sit up to get a better view.

He gently takes hold of my hand. "I told you the other day that I was helping because we need to protect each other, but the truth is that I can't stay away. I don't want to stay away."

His honesty draws the breath out of me, and heat begins to rise in my cheeks. My heart races as I lean closer and press my lips against his soft perfect mouth. I had thought that holding hands was bad enough with trying not to steal, but kissing is a whole other level. I refuse to push him away, but I can no longer focus on our embrace, and begin reinforcing my defense barriers to ensure I don't harm him.

He seems to sense my hesitation and for the first time, Vincent breaks our connection. I sit utterly still as I allow my body to relax then turn to Vincent who is looking at me with sympathetic eyes.

"This is harder than I imagined," I say.

"You don't need to excuse anything. I've made you push your boundaries enough for one night."

We don't touch again for the rest of the night, but time escapes us as we connect over some of the similarities in our childhood.

It's well into the night before we head back to the cabin.

As we make our way inside, I pause on the balcony for a second. My heart skips a beat and before I can give away too much, I grab his hand.

"I couldn't imagine going through this without you." I quickly kiss him on the cheek.

Every time I'm around him the external world ceases to exist and all I can focus on is him. I've never been so drawn to someone and the speed and intensity of what is happening should be more frightening, but my concerns slowly fade away when he's near.

Now that I have a better grasp on stealing, Vincent offers his room to me again while he takes Tyler's down the hallway.

I should go to bed, but I'm more determined than ever to get past this addiction. I wait until the house has been quiet for a short while before making my way down to the cellar. Guided by the light of the lantern, I lock myself in a cell and throw the keys out of reach.

I refuse to let anything else get in the way of Vincent and me.

I stand up tall as I regenerate. I sense the point where the energy begins to dwindle, and my body automatically goes into search mode to try and fill the empty void. Having now experienced stealing, regenerating seems to be the equivalent of going out to dinner ravenously hungry, then only eating an appetizer. Having energy shared to me is like an appetizer and main meal. Whereas stealing–my body warms at the thought–stealing is like having an eight-course meal with extras for the drive home.

So here I am, having eaten only my appetizer, and feeling utterly empty. My body begins to shake as my confinement reminds me that I have no answers in sight. I must admit, compared to how I felt after regenerating last night, tonight isn't as bad. It sparks a thought and with no other options to help, I grab onto it and set my feet firmly down.

I conjure up the ball of wind from yesterday and throw it hard against the wall. The walls down here are so thick and compact that it hardly makes a sound. *Good.*

I quickly regenerate and repeat the process over and over. Regenerate, wind ball. Regenerate, wind ball. Nine times I manage to go through the process until I can no longer regenerate enough to control air. With heavy eyelids and unsteady legs, I turn off the lantern then stagger to the bed. I flop down on top of it, sleep taking hold instantly.

CHAPTER FIFTEEN

I didn't think last night through very clearly. This morning I had to wait until Vincent woke up to let me out of my cell, then had to explain to him what I was doing down there. I didn't discuss regenerating, just brushed it off that I didn't want to risk hurting anyone overnight.

I couldn't drive away from the cabin–and my humiliation–quickly enough.

I'm mindful of the conversation with Lily yesterday and try to find her to make sure she's okay following how I left yesterday.

"Hey, how was your night?" I try and start with light conversation when I find her.

She shrugs. "Just more studying. I can't wait for today to be over."

So, she seems all right?

"Are you leaving after the exam this morning?" she asks.

I'd completely forgotten it was only a half-day to end the semester. Hallelujah! "Definitely! I might make use of the extra time and train some more."

"Want some company?" she asks quietly, not willing to look me in the eyes.

"I'm not sure if that's a good idea."

Her face drops and I try to pull the conversation back around.

"It's just that I only started regenerating again last night, so haven't recommenced training yet. I'd planned on being on my own so if I lose control and get the urge to steal, there won't be anyone there to tempt me. I wouldn't forgive myself if I hurt you in any way."

She pulls her lips into a smile. "That's all right, I should probably get ready for tonight anyway. Oh, can you tell Vince I'll see him around six o'clock?"

Vince? Tonight? The smug look on her face tells me she was waiting for a reaction, and I quickly pull myself together, so she doesn't get the satisfaction. "Not a problem. I'll let him know."

My voice must have shaken as she smirks again as she walks off.

I quickly pull out my phone and text Vincent.

What's your plans tonight?

He responds almost immediately.

Working, sorry. Expecting a huge night with Seniors finishing today.

My heart drops. He's going to be working with Lily.

I'm not going back to school next year. Technically this could be my final year to party as an 'almost' senior?

A few minutes pass as I continue staring down at the phone. I know my influence will undo what they're trying to achieve, but he said they're expecting a big night anyway so is their influence really necessary to boost orders?

Okay. But I'm bringing Tyler as backup. I'm not going to be held accountable for watching both you and Lily.

The worst part about texting is not being able to gauge emotions. I can't tell if he's angry, or making a joke, so I send back a simple smiley face.

The final exam drags on, but I am now officially done. No more exams, assignments, group projects. Ever.

I wait for Lily before I leave. We must get past this pettiness.

"Vincent's letting me come tonight to celebrate the end of the school year and Tyler's coming too. Now you're off the hook with work, why don't you hang out with us tonight and celebrate with me?"

If she's angry or surprised she doesn't let it show. "That'd be really nice."

With her sounding so sincere I try and push my luck. "I don't really have anything appropriate to wear. Any chance I can borrow something of yours? I'll come home before we head out."

She laughs. "Sure, no problems."

I really do want to try and get some training in this afternoon, so I quickly say goodbye and head back to the cabin. I had anticipated locking myself in the cell for the afternoon to train, but Vincent's already waiting for me.

"You're regenerating already?" he asks furiously as I open the door.

"Well, good day to you too, Vincent," I reply sarcastically.

"I know I pushed your boundaries yesterday but regenerating this soon after stealing isn't a good idea."

"It honestly wasn't even that bad. I could regenerate right now and control myself." I speak confidently to make my point, but thinking about last night, although I was better, it was still a struggle.

"You better hope that's true because you'll have a chance to prove it soon enough."

My eyebrows furrow. "What do you mean?"

"Lily said you were coming back here to train, and she felt I needed some extra support to help you given the seriousness of your situation."

I roll my eyes. What is she playing at?

Sure enough, within the next hour Lily turns up. Even more surprising is when Tyler also gets out of her car.

"Mad invite," Tyler jibes at Vincent.

Seriously, what is even happening?

Lily finally interjects. "I figured while Kaylee was training, we could all be here as backup in case something goes wrong, now she's crossed to the dark side." She lowers her voice when she says *dark side* for emphasis. "Plus, I figured it was good for all of us to have a game of combat to freshen up our skills," she adds with a smile.

I look at Vincent, worried. *Combat?*

"I don't think Kaylee's quite ready for combat just yet," Vincent answers on my behalf.

Lily rolls her eyes. "If you're trying to wuss out, you can verse Kaylee as a warm-up."

"Fine," Vincent responds, annoyed. "I know the perfect spot we–"

"Yeah, right here." I quickly cut him off, opening my arms out to the clearing. I hope Vincent gets the hint. That place, the plateau, it's ours. I'm not ready yet to share it with anyone else.

"Actually, here would be better." Vincent slowly nods. "Less time wasted on hiking."

I give him a smile to say *thank you,* which he reciprocates.

Before we begin combat, it's decided that I need to regenerate while the others are close by. I lock eyes with Vincent. Stealing may be my current top desire, but I know someone who's worth more to me than stealing. I open my channels and hold my breath as it reaches the maximum level I can achieve through regenerating. The energy moves in slower until it finally stops, and I squeeze my lips shut to stop a groan from escaping. I focus on Vincent, but all I can sense is that deep blue hue of his energy that's only one step away. I suddenly remember what made me give him that color in the first place. His eyes.

I stare deeply into his eyes, the same ones that had so much belief in me yesterday, and still do today. He isn't analyzing my movements. Not waiting to see if I'll crack. His confidence sends a calming sensation throughout my body. I turn my focus to my energy and decide to look at it differently. In the beginning this sensation used to feel all-encompassing and powerful, but now I'm too focused on the empty space. I look at the fulfilled space instead and concentrate on the golden energy. I recall how in the beginning I would sit and concentrate on how it moves through my body, feeling it fulfill me, ready to be utilized. I sense it now, within me, moving about with sheer strength.

I give Vincent a hesitant smile once I'm in control and he nods in approval.

Tyler moves closer to me and holds out his hand. "I'm not buying it."

Vincent smirks but nods at me to take Tyler's hand. I reach out for him without hesitation anymore. As I take his hand, rather than focusing on what he has to offer, I turn my focus inwards, seeing the overwhelming force within myself.

Then a sneaky thought pops into my head. I wait a few seconds then grab onto his arm, hard, with both my hands.

Tyler's face drops as he quickly tries to scramble away, but I throw my head back in a fit of laughter and let go of his arm.

Tyler looks at me as if I'm a crazy person but I just shrug. "I'm completely fine."

He lets out a nervous chuckle while Vincent breaks down laughing behind him. Lily hasn't moved; she just stares at us all, deeply unimpressed.

With everyone seemingly satisfied at my ability to control myself, we switch to the combat. It's decided that Tyler and Lily go first to give me a better idea of the process.

"Okay everyone," Tyler speaks with a commentary voice, "We're here to play a friendly game of combat. First round is Tyler versus Lily followed by Kaylee versus Vincent. The winners get to battle it out for the championship.

"The boundaries are contained within the clearing. You aim to disarm, not to dismember." He turns to Lily. "In one corner, we have the dark, the mysterious, the fiery Lily. Ready to take her on in the other corner is the handsome do-gooder, Tyler." Tyler gives me a wink, which earns him a scowl from Vincent.

Vincent and I make our way to the balcony as Tyler and Lily take their places, and then Vincent counts them in. As soon as he reaches *three* the action begins.

They form balls of water and fire, racing to beat the other to attack, releasing them at almost the same time. Neither finds their mark, missing by mere inches as they each move about as they try to attack. Lily creates a line of fire in front of herself, the smoke creating a screen. Tyler shoots his balls at the base of the fire, putting it out, with the last flying through the center and hitting Lily in the stomach, sending her doubled over.

She stands up straight and wipes the water off, her

piercing eyes staring him down. They both stand still for a short moment and I figure they're regenerating.

Lily quickly throws her arms forward, a spray of fire shooting in Tyler's direction. He throws a water wall up in front of him and the fire hits the wall and is pulled up into the sky.

Suddenly the water barrier falls as Tyler doubles over in a coughing fit. Behind Tyler is a thick line of fire, smoke all around him. Unable to breathe, Tyler is defenseless and throws his hands up in surrender. Lily immediately dissipates the fire and Tyler takes a moment to regain his breath.

I stare at Lily, thinking how dangerous she is. I can't imagine Tyler and Vincent enjoy training with her when they end up with smoke inhalation every time. Mind you, a lungful of water in retaliation wouldn't be the nicest either.

These three are out of my league when it comes to attacking strength.

Vincent and I move to the center of the clearing. My excitement rises as the anticipation builds.

Tyler continues to narrate the combat. "Now we move on to the battle of Vincent versus Kaylee. In the blue corner we have Kaylee, a newbie wind wielder, looking to take on the darkness who is Vincent in the red corner, a well-trained negative that has a history of being able to handle his women."

The fury in Vincent's eyes is palpable, but it just makes Tyler smile further. My stomach tenses at what Tyler is hinting at.

"Who will take out the title, the newcomer or the old favorite?"

Tyler and Lily retreat to the safety of the balcony, and Tyler continues his monologue, shouting out to the field. "Is everyone ready to get started?"

Tyler looks at Vincent and me and we both nod.

"On the count of three. One..."

Vincent gives me a cheeky grin.

"Two..."

I poke out my tongue.

"Three!"

I already had a grasp on some wind, so as soon as I'm able I throw my arm forward. A tunnel of wind flies forward and hits Vincent in the chest, knocking him back as I had done to Tyler the other day.

Tyler starts clapping and shouting, "That's my girl."

I take the opportunity to quickly regenerate. Vincent brushes the dirt off himself then gives me a nod as if to say he understands I can hold my own, and the battle recommences.

There's no wind blowing so I start running, feeling the air flow over my body. I stumble on a pile of rocks in the process, knowing full well it's one of Vincent's dirty tricks. I fall hard to the ground. Next thing I know, a pile of dirt starts flying directly for me. I swing my left arm down to the ground in a counterclockwise direction and focus on the air my arm is flowing through, hoping to start a thread. It builds just in time and the whirlwind encases me. The mud hits soon after and is sprayed off to the left.

Vincent gives me his perfect smile.

I take the moment to regenerate again, and once I've topped my energy up, I swing both arms down then forward, throwing the wind toward Vincent. This time it moves over the ground like a wave heading straight for him and there's no way he can outrun it. I've won!

Just before it hits him, Vincent ducks and a mound of earth builds over the top of him like an igloo. The wave flows over the top, completely missing him.

In anticipation of his next attack, I know I need to build a defense but instead of a whirlwind I have another idea based on what just occurred. I wave both my hands forward and upwards and create a wall in front of me, shielding me from the incoming rain of mud and dirt. I'm feeling impressed by myself at this point, wondering what I can try next. A tickling sensation runs over my feet and I look down to weeds growing over them! I send a wave of wind across the ground and all the weeds are cut off, freeing me.

I'm trying to figure out my next attack when I'm grabbed from behind in a bear hug and my wind wall dissipates. Arms made from weeds hug around my body and I can't move.

Vincent loads up a large ball of dirt and propels it forward. My heart races as it draws nearer, knowing I'm unable to protect myself. It stops just shy of my nose and I let out a long breath as I stare at the ball that's as wide as my shoulders.

"Ladies and gentlemen, we have our winner, old time favorite Vincent, the earth mover," Tyler announces as they make their way toward us.

When the weeds slacken off, I turn around to see what he had created. A figure of Vincent is standing in front of me, made from weeds. I can't hold in my laugh.

I walk over to Vincent and shake his hand. "You win again, but be warned, it only makes me train harder."

"That was seriously amazing, Kaylee," he replies. "I can't believe you learned to do all that within the week!"

"I figured out the whirlwind barrier and tunnel strike attack the other day but played around with the wall shield just then. It's funny what you come up with in the moment." I'm feeling rather proud of myself, although utterly exhausted.

"With the closing of the second round, we come to the grand finale." Tyler begins his monologue. "Who would have thought the two negatives would end up facing each other?"

As the action begins, Vincent and Lily move seamlessly against one another, each knowing the other's strengths and weaknesses. One attacks while the other defends and vice versa. You can tell the hours they've spent working together. The history. It's mesmerizing but an unfamiliar feeling courses through me. Jealousy? She told me nothing had happened between them but now I'm not sure. You don't spend that amount of time with someone without getting attached. I know firsthand what can occur in a single week alone.

Suddenly Lily's foot catches on a mound of debris that Vincent has planted around her. She falls to the ground, and when she stands her knees are grazed and bleeding. She raises her hands above her head, arching her back. Vincent stopped attacking when she fell, but the moment she arches, he throws up an igloo twice the size of the one he made with my attack.

Lily propels her arms forward and a wide burst of flame shoots in Vincent's direction, flowing over his igloo. It pours out of her with unyielding magnitude. It dawns on me that the attacks Vincent, Tyler, and I have been using can leave bruises, but one touch from Lily's attack and we'll be left with burned skin, or worse. Her attack is relentless. Five seconds, ten seconds, fifteen seconds. I begin to worry, wondering how thick the walls are. Or has Vincent just created a human oven? I look to Tyler who gives me a worrying glance.

There's no way for Vincent signaling he's not okay, and he only just finished combat with me. What if his energy has fully drained? I begin to panic, seeing the strength of fire continue from Lily, and a strong sensation churns through my stomach that I need to act. Now.

"Stop!" I shout out, but she can't hear me.

I run down the stairs and throw my arms forward. A tunnel of wind heads straight for Lily. It hits her in the side of the leg, and she buckles over in pain, the fire retreating in the process.

She stares at me with piercing eyes. "What the hell?" Lily begins, but I ignore her as I throw another tunnel at Vincent's shield with all the strength in my body.

It leaves a gaping hole in the barrier and not long after, Vincent steps into view. He's flushed and sweating but looks all right.

I let out a sigh of relief.

"What happened?" Vincent asks.

"I–" my voice cracks. "I couldn't tell if you were okay."

"Oh, Kaylee," he says and wraps his arms around me.

The adrenaline is still coursing through my body and my emotions are a mess. As soon as I'm in his arms my whole body relaxes.

"So, does that mean Lily wins by default?" Tyler finally adds to try and lighten the mood.

Lily doesn't even acknowledge her achievement. She continues to stare wide-eyed at Vincent and me and as soon as I lock eyes with her, she drops her gaze to the ground. She'd taken the hint that I've fallen for him, but I don't think she realized that the feelings were this strong or reciprocated.

The change in atmosphere ends the combat training and with the heavy tension between us all, we decide it's best to go our separate ways to start preparations for tonight's party.

CHAPTER SIXTEEN

Vincent and Tyler head back to their apartment so they can quickly get ready then help with finishing the set up at the club. I tried to ask specifics, but Vincent doesn't want me involved. He told me he hates having to drag Lily into it as it is.

I take the opportunity to use the shower before Lily hogs the bathroom.

When I walk back to Vincent's room, lying on the bed is a dress I forgot I even had. I was supposed to wear it to the Sophomore dance last year, but we moved before I had the chance. Mom had picked it out for me. It's a royal blue strapless dress which flares out from the waist and stops just shy of the knees. Mom thought the corset bust section would give me an extra lift to compensate for my late blooming, but now I've filled out, it fits perfectly. The silk material rubs against my skin and it feels foreign. I'm usually not a dress type of person.

I take the time to put my hair up in a neat bun and apply some simple makeup. I've never really worn makeup so whenever I try something fancy it ends up looking like a hot mess.

I walk laps of the hallway as my excitement builds for tonight. Lily finally emerges from the bathroom and the first thing I notice is how grown up she looks. She's been wearing makeup for the last few years so the combination of eyebrow shaping, and cheek contouring make her face look mature beyond her years. Her long curly brown hair frames her face and upper body, and her womanly curves are on display in a form-fitting black crop top and waist high skirt. She's the image of a typical partygoer. Not that age matters where we're going.

"You didn't need to borrow anything of mine after all." Lily gives me a small smile.

I look down at my dress, which now seems to highlight my youth in comparison to her. "Thanks. I didn't realize I still had it."

"Well, we should probably leave, otherwise they'll think we've bailed on them," she informs me.

I roll my eyes. I'd almost be there by now if I hadn't had to wait for her.

We drive in silence, but Lily is gnawing on her lip, a tell-tale sign she has something to say.

"Spit it out." I've been waiting for this conversation since this afternoon.

She shakes her head. "It's nothing, really."

I stare at her, unmoving. She may be driving, but I know in her peripherals she can see me waiting.

"You really like him, don't you?"

There it is. "I really do."

"He's not a good choice for you."

"And you're supposed to know what's best for me?" I reply sharply. She flinches and I'm automatically riddled with guilt. "He's been nothing but nice to me," I try to reassure her.

"That's because you've only known him a week."

She's been so anti-Vincent since the beginning. There must be more to the story than she's letting on. "Did something happen between the two of you?" I ask again.

She takes a moment before responding. "I spent months with Vincent and Tyler when I was training and that opened me up to caring for them both greatly. But all it took was one night out working with Vincent to see him for who he really is."

She gave me that same spiel earlier. I wait for her to explain but I can't tell if she's deep in thought or has finished. "Who is he then?"

"You know the sole purpose of his job is to heighten people's abilities to let loose and buy more alcohol, right? That should be clue enough to his character. But to make it worse, letting loose also means these people lose their sexual inhibitions. Vincent's a good-looking guy, so it's not hard to believe that the whole night he has women, and even the odd man, hanging off him to compete for his attention. He goes from entertaining one person to the next multiple times during the night because he can. They're basically an endless selection for him to pick and choose from until he's had his fill."

That's rich, coming from her. She goes to the club too to lower people's inhibitions. But at the same time, I know what she's saying is true. I saw it firsthand the night I met Vincent, how everyone gravitated to him, and at Brittany's house party last week. But he also brushed Brittany off. Was that because of me? Or was he just not interested in her? "He hasn't given me any indication not to trust him, so the least I can do is give him the benefit of the doubt."

She shakes her head. "Maybe his true character will reveal itself to you sooner than anticipated."

The car begins to slow down as she pulls into a driveway. She parks beside Vincent's pickup at the back of a building and leads me round to the front. Déjà vu overwhelms me when the stale putrid smell infiltrates my nostrils as we enter the lonely bar that flipped my whole world upside down.

Sure enough, there behind the counter is the same big, gruff barman from last time.

"Hi Frank," Lily says with charm.

Without missing a beat, Frank addresses me. "I never forget a face. No invite, no entry."

"Kaylee Saunders." I grin at Frank. Vincent said he'd add me to the list this time.

Lily doesn't wait for his instructions before heading around the side of the counter, letting herself into the walk-in cooler. I quickly follow her, not wanting to be left alone with Frank.

As we exit the walk-in cooler, the intense vibration from the beat of the music radiates through me and my palms start to sweat as I recall the ending of last time.

"You need a drink!" Lily shouts to me, wide-eyed.

I nod. This is supposed to be a celebration of us finishing the school year, not me being an anxious wreck.

We wind our way through the crowd and find a vacant spot at the bar. Another familiar face greets us as Sam ignores the rest of the crowd to serve us.

"Nice to see you again, Kaylee." He gives me a charming smile, then quickly adds in, "And you too, Lily. What will it be, ladies?"

Lily rolls her eyes. "Something sweet and strong,"

He raises his eyebrows at her but doesn't comment on her harsh tone. He goes to work, grabbing over half a dozen bottles, then hands us each a concoction that is yellow on the bottom and blue on top. Lily swirls her straw around and the mixture turns a light green color. I follow her lead and take a sip of the sickly-sweet drink. So sweet, that I can hardly taste the alcohol. I've found my drink for the night!

I pull out my wallet to pay, but Sam just waves his hand and moves on to the next person. I smile at his generosity.

Lily leads me away from the bar and passes through the crowded dance floor. We finally emerge on the other side to some booths. They all seem to be taken, but Lily keeps walking, the sound of the music lowering ever so slightly as we make our way to the back. She leads me to the rear corner where a booth is sectioned off. She removes the rope and sits down.

I wait for someone to tell us off, but she quickly laughs.

"I like to make sure I have somewhere to get away if I'm having a crappy night. There's no rule stating I have to enjoy my time here; only my presence is needed."

I must admit, I was annoyed at Lily being allowed out to work, but I've never seen her hungover, so I wonder if she always came to these events sober. I can't imagine she had much fun spending hours here surrounded by drunken teenagers. Does Vincent feel the same way? Lily sure doesn't seem to think so.

My body seems to sense their energy close by and I look around until I find them. I catch sight of Tyler first. He walks with a quiet confidence in his step and a smile that could make any woman weak at the knees. He's not putting on an act, it's just a quality that seems to exude without him even trying. He reaches up and strokes the short patch of hair on the underside of his chin.

Then I spot Vincent. People try to stop him the way they did last week but this time he just nods in acknowledgment and continues walking, his attention glued to me. I hope Lily is watching.

His gaze makes its way from my feet to my eyes and he gives me a breathtaking smile. I can almost palpate the longing behind it. Tonight, he's replaced his usual black party attire with some navy jeans and a light blue button up shirt. He looks ravishing.

He reaches the booth and we both take the side opposite Lily and Tyler. As we sit, he wraps his arm around my waist, drawing me closer to him. His lips press into my neck, then he inhales, giving my waist a gentle squeeze as he lets out a small groan. Despite knowing that the music would have drowned out the sound to anyone else, it still sends a wave of heat up my neck, and I try to calm my mind to prevent my face from beaming bright red. I can say with certainty that the hunger for stealing has well and truly subsided.

"Looking lovely, ladies," he addresses Lily and me, but refuses to take his eyes off me.

He's never been so forward with me, and especially not in public, so it takes me a moment to gather myself.

"Tyler." Lily gives him a nod. "Vincent." She adds on his name, half-hearted.

I grab my drink and take a few big mouthfuls, thankful for any distraction to take me away from the tension growing around the table. The noise of the straw sucking up air takes me by surprise.

"You might want to pace yourself." Lily raises her eyebrows at me. Her drink is still full.

"I'll keep an eye on her," Vincent says with a grin, which causes Lily to roll her eyes.

"Let's dance." He looks at me with pleading eyes, and half drags me out of the booth before I have a chance to respond.

Lily and Tyler don't follow, and I'm thankful for the time

alone with Vincent. I haven't had a chance to be alone with him since the desire to steal has settled.

We make our way onto the dance floor and my stomach drops. I don't dance. Most people, including Vincent, are just stepping side to side to the beat and it takes me a second to synchronize my steps with them. The over-crowdedness of the dance floor eventually pushes us closer together and Vincent grabs onto both of my hands and guides them over his shoulders. He wraps his hands around my waist, and we continue to sway to the music, despite it being the wrong sort of dancing for the upbeat music playing. The proximity between us closes ever so slowly until we're basically pressed up against each other.

"You look divine." He talks into my ear so I can hear over the music, and then pulls back to gaze at me with longing.

"You're in a good mood!" I shout back with a chuckle.

"I just don't want to waste any more time," he states seriously.

Does this sudden forwardness have anything to do with how he opened up last night? We both lowered our defenses yesterday.

He grabs my hands from behind his neck and spins me halfway around. He lowers our hands together in front of me, then hugs me back into him. We continue to sway to the music, and he plants a gentle kiss on the back of my neck.

I let myself get lost in the movement with him, enjoying the proximity. The beat of the music drowns out any thoughts running through my mind, so I finally get to be present without over-thinking. I rest my head back against his shoulder and close my eyes as we dance together, taking in the warmth of his body pressed against my back.

As we continue to dance, my body stops responding as quickly as usual, and I blink a few times to try and focus against the dizziness. I really care about Vincent, but the last thing I want is to lose my inhibitions because of alcohol.

I turn around and shout in his ear, "I'm getting a bit hot. I think I might go grab some water."

"I'll get you some. Why don't you go and wait at the booth?" He turns and heads for the bar.

I make my way back to where Lily is sitting alone. Her arms are folded as she sits slumped in the booth, obviously unimpressed with this evening. She still hasn't touched her drink.

"Want to come and dance?" I ask, trying to involve her in this evening.

"No, I'm good here."

"Want some company?" I try again, sitting down across from her.

She gives me a smirk. "No, you'd better make use of your last few days together."

I can tell she's trying to get me to bite, but this time I'm clueless as to what she's talking about. "What do you mean?"

"You're so naïve," she says, shaking her head.

"What is your problem?" I finally let out, fed up with her negativity. "Are you jealous that Vincent chose me over you? Or that I can be happy without you? What is it?"

"You know what, I was hoping that Vincent would be the one to step up and let you down gently, but I guess I'll be the grown up here. What the hell are you two thinking? Have you honestly not looked into the future and thought *hmmm maybe this isn't a good idea?* I'm not pissed that Vincent didn't take a second glance my way because I was smart enough to know that nothing would ever eventuate. Let's start with the simple fact that Vincent's leaving in a week to join your mom, and even if he wasn't, in one month's time we won't even live in this damned place!"

I pause and for the first time this week I think beyond the present moment. We're moving soon. And Vincent's leaving in a week? To join Mom? But I don't have time to think about it because Lily's tirade isn't over.

"I mean, sure he'll visit because of Pop, but that'll be what? Two, maybe three times a year?" She places her hand on her chin and exaggerates a thinking face as she speaks. "And let's say for fun that you both somehow manage to get around a long-distance relationship. Are you going to eventually create your own pair, and then I'll be left paired with Tyler? Knowing Vincent and Tyler's history, do you really think it's going to be so easy for Vincent to leave him? And have you even thought what that would look like in terms of basically never seeing Mom and me again?

"And then what? You finally become a pair, but what's going to happen when you can't have children together but need to continue the line? Are you seriously going to be happy knowing that someone else is carrying Vincent's child, and you'll be carrying your own child that doesn't belong to him?" Her shoulders heave up and down as she lets her frustration out.

The wind has been knocked out of me and I'm finding it hard to concentrate. Long-distance hadn't even crossed my mind. And I'm only seventeen so of course I haven't thought much about children, but what does she mean about not being able to have children together?

It's as if she can read the confusion on my face and she shakes her head. "Of course he didn't tell you. Why would he? He's so caught up in getting what he wants from you in this moment that he's too cowardly to tell you the truth. You're not the first pair to try and have a relationship, but none of the active eight have ever been able to have children together."

Now that her frustration has been released, she reads my overwhelmed face and covers her mouth in shock. She reaches across the table to grab my hand, but I lean back out of reach. Right now, my head is spinning with information and I just want to be left alone.

"I'm not the bad person here, Kaylee." She exits the booth, leaving me to my thoughts.

It might not be her fault that Vincent hasn't divulged these truths, but the jealousy is laced in her words. She has obviously thought a lot about this type of situation long before I became a factor with Vincent. She could have said something on the drive, or any other time this week but she's specifically waited until I was at the peak of my happiness.

But at the end of the day, this relationship between Vincent and me has nothing to do with her. Has he purposely been keeping this information from me?

It's hard not to crumple into a ball. How could I be so stupid? I was so blinded by infatuation that I didn't even think about us moving. It also reinforces the fact that for the rest of my life I'm going to be paired to another person, and I must get used to thinking about someone else's—well Lily's—needs as well as my own. And children? I know at some point I want children, but I never thought I'd have to consider it now. My mind can't focus. I place my elbows on the table and lean my head into my hands, trying to find some clarity in thought.

And Vincent! I'm feeling so betrayed. If he knew we only had two weeks together, what was the point in starting anything? Was I just some entertainment to fill the time as Lily has been saying all along? And he's going to join the hunt for XET? He obviously has a death wish, knowing that one of the fighters was killed recently. He's only nineteen, so how can they let him get involved?

Before I have a chance to collect my thoughts, gentle hands grab my forearms. I lift my head out of my hands and stare into the face I've come to cherish, but this time I can't smile.

His eyebrows are furrowed with worry, but he doesn't speak.

"You're leaving in a week?" I try to hide the sorrow in my face, but I fail.

His gaze shifts down to the table. "We're supposed to leave next weekend, but I was going to see if I could stay for a little while longer. We're making great progress with your training, and Pop could use a hand getting started with packing up."

So, he can admit he wants to stay to help me train but nothing more? This isn't the time to be vague about feelings. "What are we doing, Vincent? You're leaving. I'm moving away. What was the whole purpose of whatever this is between us? You said before that you didn't want to waste any more time and have been so direct today. Is that because you know you have limited time left to try and get in my pants?"

I don't know where the last statement came from, and I'm horrified that it escaped. I can tell it stings him. But now that it's out, it hurts just as much to even consider that might be his motivation.

"The purpose is that I care about you, and for once in my life I can actually be myself around someone without worrying what their true intentions are," he responds with a firm tone.

"Great, so I'm only good to you because I can't be influenced by you?"

He rubs the back of his neck. "I gave up on relationships a long time ago because I was never certain of the intentions behind a person staying with me. Then I met you. You know we had a connection right from the start. And then I realized I'd never have to worry about my influence with you, so I did something selfish and I ignored everything else. And I'm sorry I made that choice, but at the same time I'm not because for once in my life I finally have something with someone that comes so effortlessly, and I know that it's real."

I can feel a lump forming at the back of my throat as water wells in my eyes. "But at what cost? Was this always supposed to be a summertime fling for you? I can't speak for you, but I'm not that sort of person, Vincent. I admit I hadn't even thought of the next few months, and I'm not saying that's your fault, but this should have been a discussion we had earlier."

He shakes his head and shrugs. "I didn't come into this with an expectation for length of time. All I knew was that every day I woke up I wanted to spend more time with you, so I did. And now that I'm supposed to be leaving, I find myself trying to make any excuse not to go."

In any other circumstance I'd be elated about his words, but now they bring nothing but sadness.

"But you are leaving." I sound more heartbroken than I intend.

"I have to. They need more people at Headquarters. XET are planning something, but they don't have enough eyes watching them."

"You could be killed!" I stress.

"And if I don't go, then a lot more of us could be. You could be."

I sit still staring at him. I'm furious. "What is it with everyone putting their life on the line to spare mine? Where's my choice in all of this to protect myself? If you're leaving, then just go already. I don't need you for training and Pop's fine without you."

"Kaylee," he says softly, reaching out for me.

"No!" I stand up and yank my hand away. "I'm not sticking around to fall more in love with you, only for you to go off and risk your life. That's not fair."

The air hangs heavy around us. There it is, laid on the table. I've fallen in love with him.

"Kaylee," he tries again, rising out of his seat.

My vision blurs as the tears start to come but I don't want him to see it. "Please, Vincent. There's no point dragging out the inevitable."

He pauses for a second and I take a step away from the table. Some part of me wishes he'll reach out for me, but the other part knows I need to go. He doesn't move. My lip quivers as I turn away. I don't make it far before Lily links her arm around mine and this time, I lean into her for support as she guides me through the crowds and out of the pub. My body is shaking, but I won't let the tears come yet. Inside I'm numb, and I focus on that feeling, because it's a hell of a lot better than the other feelings threatening to seep through.

I get into the passenger seat and curl myself into a ball, leaning against the door. Lily remains silent the whole drive as I focus on the streetlights flashing by one after another. Anything to keep my mind occupied from my heartbreak.

My body recognizes the familiarity of the turns we make as we get close to home, and I stare out into the night as our house emerges. I've been gone a week, but this place already feels foreign.

Lily lets me into the house and locks up behind me.

"Goodnight," she says quietly as we reach the top of the staircase.

I don't respond. Not to be rude, but because if I make any

other sound, I'll break down before I reach my door. As I make those final steps toward my room, it becomes hard to swallow as my throat tightens and my vision blurs. I reach my hand out for the wall and use the corridor as a guide. With the click of my door closing, my legs go weak and I press my back against the door, sliding down to the floor. I hug my legs in tightly and press my forehead into my knees. My mouth opens wide and my throat tightens as I let out a silent scream, my body shaking as I expel my suffering.

Tears finally make their way down my face and it takes all my might to hold in the sound of the sobs. I rock back against the door and my zipper digs into my back. The pain drags me from my despair, and I welcome that distraction. I press harder against the door. As I rock back again for a third time, my back thuds loudly and I pause, waiting for any noise from Lily or Aunt Amy's rooms.

The sudden change in atmosphere awakens me to what I'm doing, and I attempt to pull myself together. I change for bed and stare at the dress on the floor. I never want to see it again. As I shove it in the back of my closet, a piece of black clothing captures my attention and with shaking hands, I pull the jacket out and lift the collar to my face. It still smells of him. I turn off the light and curl up in bed, hugging Vincent's jacket. I gently rock myself as I let the emotions pour out as silently as possible, eventually making myself too exhausted to keep my eyes open any longer.

CHAPTER SEVENTEEN

My eyelids scratch against dry eyes as I attempt to adjust to the morning light. Following closely is a thumping beat radiating through my forehead as if I'm waking from a hangover. But I'm not hungover. My body is emotionally drained. As last night's memories flood through me, the pain in my chest overcomes all other senses. I scramble for my phone, some sliver of hope to see if Vincent has reached out. The only thing the screen tells me is that I've slept till lunch time.

What have I done? I'd welcome the tears now, just to provide some relief to my eyes, but my body doesn't have any left.

I curl back up in bed, hugging his jacket. How had I been so blinded by my feelings for him that I didn't even think about us leaving? Even if he wasn't going to Headquarters, he still isn't allowed to be around me for long periods of time. He even said that different pairs can't remain around each other for long when he was teaching me. Why didn't either of us pick up on that sooner?

I told him I loved him. I think I've known it since the moment we met. I'd never been so instantly drawn to someone in my life and hadn't been able to get him out of my head from that moment on. Every touch induced an electric current, as if the world was giving me a sign that this was the person for me.

How am I supposed to move on when I don't want it to end? The thought of never seeing him again makes my heart ache. Not being able to hold those gentle hands. Kiss those soft lips.

He never tried to stop me from leaving, though. Had it been so simple for him just to let things end there? Maybe I was just a quick fling to him? My stomach knots at the thought.

I sit up on the edge of the bed, my back slumped as my body struggles to find the strength to keep me upright. My reflection stares back at me in the mirror on my dresser. I almost look as bad as I feel. Despite a full night's sleep, dark rings encompass bloodshot eyes, further emphasized by my pale face. I should eat something. But that would mean going downstairs and facing Lily and Aunt Amy.

Where do I even start with that conversation?

It's too much to think about for now, so I decide on a shower to try and freshen up. As the water rushes over my head, the outside world drowns out and I'm left with a sound that reminds me of rain hitting a roof. It offers a sense of calming and I let out a deep sigh. Surely this can't be the right decision if I'm feeling this horrible. But what other option is there? Vincent has obviously made up his mind to leave with Tyler. And now I've realized that having a rela-tionship will directly impact Tyler and Lily, can we be that selfish to eventually create a new pair? Would he even be willing to separate from Tyler given they've been each other's main support for so long? And if he is willing to be with me, it would also mean needing to have children with other people. How do you even begin that discussion as teenagers?

I shake my head. It doesn't matter. Vincent is leaving and there's a high chance that something horrible could happen to him. A pang of nausea courses through my stomach. I hate thinking of worst-case scenarios, but years of believing my mother was fighting in the army has developed a thick skin to reality. And this is the new reality. That two of the most important people in my life are putting their lives at risk for my safety.

I feel so utterly useless.

So, what now? Am I supposed to go back to my day-to-day activities, forget about Vincent, forget about my gifts and be a regular teenager? I don't think I have that in me. I know too much. I also know I'm too weak to fight against XET. Is that something I could see in my future? Joining the fight? I don't feel I can live a normal life while XET exists, so maybe this could be my future?

And Vincent would be there.

My heart quickly flutters.

Last night, everything felt so sudden and heightened, but now after some time to think...? I quickly pause before my thoughts run away. I need to talk to the other person in this equation. Lily. I must understand that she is a part of my life whether I like it or not and try to gauge what she plans on doing coming into her final year of school and beyond.

I get out of the shower, feeling excited. I'd never thought about what I wanted to do after high school, but now I have a purpose. I get dressed, tidy my face and hair, and while there are still remnants of last night's heartbreak evident on my face, it's greatly improved since I last looked in the mirror.

My palms begin to sweat as I make my way downstairs. Despite my planned discussion with Lily and Aunt Amy, I still need to apologize for the last week. I make my way into the kitchen and they're both sitting at the dining room table. Aunt Amy has always been on the thinner side, but in comparison to her well-proportioned daughter, her frail frame and hollow eyes send a pang of guilt through me. Her dark brown hair sits neatly in a bob above her shoulders, but it makes her usually pale skin seem almost translucent. Have I been the cause of her stress? I forget that she too hasn't been without me for a long period of time and I just forced it upon her.

Aunt Amy tries to speak, but I hold my hand up to stop her. "Please let me say something first. I'm really sorry about my behavior this last week. It wasn't right of me to not come home one night and then to make no contact whatsoever. And I also appreciate everything the both of you have done for me while Mom hasn't been here. I know we're not related by blood, but you will always be my family." The words flow out of me faster than usual and I try to release the tension in my shoulders to calm my nerves. My whole body is rigid.

Aunt Amy reaches over and takes my hand. "You have nothing to apologize for. I mean yes, it would have been nice to hear straight from you that you weren't coming back home for a while, but at the same time we understand what it's like to have all this information revealed. You forget that I was never part of this world until I met Tom, and Lily only found out a few years ago. We know what it's like to react to that sort of news. We just want to make sure that you're okay."

Her statement brings me to the brink of tears. I get up and give Aunt Amy a hug and my whole body finally relaxes. Lily's eyes are glistening like mine. We both smile and hug too.

"There is something I'd like to discuss." My stomach

knots. "I would like to join Headquarters in the fight against XET."

Aunt Amy's face drops in horror, and Lily just shakes her head.

"This is because of Vincent isn't it?" Lily says in a frustrated tone.

"No!" I quickly reassure her. Well, not totally. "I've known for the last week that I wouldn't be going back to school. I just don't see the point when there's so much more going on in our lives."

"The point is," Aunt Amy cuts in, "that your mother has sacrificed all her time and effort to give you the life she never had. You've only just started learning your skills so you will be more of a hindrance than an asset at the moment."

"I know that right now I'm not of any use, but I figured Lily would still be going to school for senior year and I can use that time to train. And I could get a job to help pay for myself and toward Pop now that Vin–" it's hard to mention his name without my voice breaking, "Vincent and Tyler are going. By the end of next year, I'll be eighteen, and can join Mom, and Lily might have a better idea of what she wants to do following high school. She could study or work nearby so we could still be paired." It all flows out of me. I hadn't even thought of half of this before right now, but as the words escape it all makes sense.

"Look." Aunt Amy's addressing me more firmly than I'm used to hearing. "As you said, you need time, so let's just focus on moving first. Then, once we're settled, you can speak to your mother about your ideas of not returning to school. If she's on board then we can discuss this all later."

It's not a yes, but it's also not a no. I smile and nod in agreement. Surely Mom can't be that much of a hypocrite and stop me from joining her?

With my appetite returning, I help myself to some food. Lily's still waiting at the table when I return.

"You might be fooling her, but I know this is about Vincent. After everything we spoke about last night, you still haven't let go of the idea of the two of you together?"

"If I was so hung up on the idea of Vincent and me, why would I be willing to wait a whole year before joining Headquarters?"

"You know he's left already, don't you? I told you he didn't care." She says it in the snide voice that poured out last night during her tirade.

It's as if she's punched me in the stomach. *He's already left?* "But what about his work and Pop?" I ask, grasping at straws.

"Last night was the last event booked and they said they'd come back in a few weeks to help Pop to pack. There was no other reason to stay."

Did I mean that little to him that he couldn't even say goodbye? I know I told him to go, but this just feels as though he's wiping his hands clean of me. I don't believe her.

I look over to the key bowl and sure enough Aunt Amy's car keys are in there. Without hesitation, I grab the keys and head out the door. Lily doesn't even bother following me.

But where am I going? I don't know where Tyler and Vincent have been staying, so I head toward the only place I can think of; Pop's cabin. I drive as fast as I can, knowing that if I spend one second longer in the car alone with my thoughts, I'll crumble.

Maybe I had it all wrong? We've known one another a week, so maybe I wasn't as important to him as he is to me? Maybe I scared him off when I told him I loved him? Did he honestly think that I wanted him to leave? I know when I said it to him, I meant it, but that was in the heat of the moment.

Couples fight all the time, don't they? But that doesn't mean they run away without a second thought.

The bumps of the dirt road shake me out of my thoughts, and I slow down to make sure I get to Pop's in one piece. As the cabin comes into view, I hold my breath, hoping to see Vincent's pickup, or even just Pop.

I don't seem to be in luck. The cabin is unlocked as usual and as I have no other option but to wait, I figure I may as well pack my stuff up while I'm here. All my items are still sprawled around Vincent's room.

Midway through cleaning, I hear footsteps coming from the front of the house.

"Vincent?" I call out in hope.

"Kaylee?" returns the deep husky voice I've come to know as Pop.

My heart drops.

I walk out to greet him, and the moment my eyes meet his, all I can see is Vincent staring back at me.

"He's gone, hasn't he?" I half choke on a sob as the words escape.

"Oh, child." He stretches his arms open and I run into his embrace, burying my face in his chest. His strong arms hold me tight as my body drains itself of emotion again.

"He didn't even say goodbye," I finally manage to let out, tears beginning to fall down my cheeks. "I panicked and told him to go, all because I was scared. He was leaving anyway, and I can't expect him to separate from Tyler to create a new pair with me. We can't even have kids of our own." It all comes pouring out and I'm expecting Pop to laugh because of my age and the fact I've known Vincent for a week.

"Come and sit down, won't you?" he requests. "Did I ever tell you how my daughter ended up paired to her soulmate, Sarah?"

I shake my head to indicate he hasn't.

"My Sophia and your mother were paired until they were nineteen years old. At that time, there was already one pair with children, and not long afterward, a positive from another pair impregnated his girlfriend. This created a problem, though, as he was only seventeen years old, so it wasn't fair to expect his pair–Lily's father, Tom, who was sixteen at the time–to think about creating a family.

"Other than your mom and Sophia, the only other pair was Cody and Sarah. The four of them gathered to work out who would be the best suitor, as there always needs to be a balance with children. Fortunately, Cody was in a long-standing relationship and they agreed to begin a family, so he paired with the seventeen-year-old.

"Their other halves, Tom and Sarah, were supposed to create a new pair, but the moment Sarah and Sophia met, they fell in love. Because Sarah was a positive and Sophia was negative, they were able to create a new pair and as a result, your mom and Lily's father ended up pairing.

"Even though we always try to keep pairs together as long as possible, it's not always the case because not everyone is ready to have families at the same point in time. Do you think you'll forgive yourself if you choose Lily's happiness over your own when you may not even be a part of each other's lives in a few years' time?"

I'd never considered that Lily and I could be separated anyway in the coming years. The same could be said for Vincent and Tyler. If that happened, I'd always regret not taking the chance with Vincent in creating a new pair. But does he even want me after last night? What about having a family?

"Is it true that pairs can't have children with one another?"

I ask Pop. The only person I've heard that coming from is Lily, so I want to make sure she wasn't lying.

"Yes, that's correct; they can't. Charlotte knew her gift had to be spread between multiple people because no human has the strength to hold two elements. Despite trying, pairs have never been able to conceive because the combination of their genes isn't compatible with life.

"I'll ask you a question though. Do you think Vincent sees his brother as a half-brother? Or that he didn't think of both of his mothers as true mothers?"

I mull over his question and shake my head no.

"I know Sophia and Sarah are different because they would never have been able to physically have children together, but if they were so hung up on the idea that their partner would have a child that wasn't biologically theirs, then Vincent and Tyler wouldn't exist. Vincent has been brought up in an environment where it never would have crossed his mind that it would be a problem if a partner of his couldn't carry his child. There's also never a guarantee in life that you will be able to conceive anyway, so how do you think you would have proceeded in the case of infertility? If you really loved someone, do you think it would even be an option to break up, just because you wouldn't have biological children together?"

This topic is well beyond my comfort zone. Apart from knowing I wanted children at some point, I've never thought much into infertility or cared about someone enough to think about our future with children. But now that it's laid out on the table, I can't believe I allowed that point from Lily to be a factor in last night's argument with Vincent. I allow my emotions too much hold on me. I wouldn't be in this situation had I thought things through before speaking with Vincent.

"I think I've ruined everything," I finally admit, as a gut-wrenching pain courses through me. "He's gone. We're leaving. And I've made him so angry with me."

"When things are meant to be, they'll find a way of working themselves out." He gives my hand a gentle squeeze and leaves me alone with my sorrow.

It wasn't the reassuring statement that I was hoping for. But what was I expecting? That everything was going to be fine and that Vincent was magically going to reappear and tell me he loved me too and wanted to create a new pair?

If fighting with Headquarters is what he genuinely wants, and it's what I want too, then maybe I should follow Pop's advice and let the future work itself out. Once I'm trained and am in a position to join Headquarters, then who knows what might happen? I said it last night, that I've fallen in love with Vincent, but we have only known each other a week, so I can't expect him to create a new pair and give up this pursuit in fighting XET just for me. I want to make sure if we're going to do this, that we have had more time and not made a rash decision as this choice will affect so many lives. That means I'm moving with Lily, Aunt Amy, and Pop, that I commit myself to training, and when the time comes, I hope with all my heart that Vincent still wants to be with me. That is, if I'm correct in thinking he feels the same way about me.

CHAPTER EIGHTEEN

Three weeks have passed and neither Vincent nor I have reached out to one another. I want to apologize, but that needs to be done in person, plus I'm sure he's being kept busy. Also, I'd never forgive myself if he were preoccupied with something going on between the two of us and gets injured by XET.

Aunt Amy was finally offered a position in a small town in Wisconsin that is close to a forest–for Pop–so we move in two days. It's funny, because I'd always hated moving, but now, I can't wait to leave this place. I will always remember that this town turned my world upside down, and as empowering and wonderful as regeneration and using my gifts are, I wonder if I would have chosen to find out if I'd had a choice. I realize it's a question I'm going to have to ask myself for my future child too.

This is the place that I grew to love someone besides family for the first time, only to have him ripped from my life. The pain of not being able to be wrapped in his arms, and of not having him to confide in, is so overwhelming at times that I've had to ban myself from thinking about him.

Almost every day, Lily and I have gone out to Pop's to train. She hasn't said anything more about my plans for the next year, or about Vincent and me, so for the most part we're getting along well again. I'm getting stronger each day with controlling my air element, and I've also started martial arts training. Aunt Amy has helped to pay for lessons, so I've been able to go to three classes a week.

"What are you thinking about?" Lily inquires. We've dropped in for a smoothie at a local cafe after our day of training.

"Just that I need to find a new martial arts instructor after the move."

"Maybe I can come to a few lessons?" she asks enthusiastically.

I smile and nod. It'd be nice to learn skills together so we can work on physical combat as well as element work when we train.

"Kaylee?" a voice says from behind me.

I turn around, trying to find a familiar face. It takes a second to register the tall, stocky person speaking to me.

"Hi Sam," I reply with surprise. The last time I saw him was when he was working behind the bar the night Vincent and I had the argument. I quickly shove that thought inside. "What're you doing here?"

"Just grabbing some energy." He holds up his coffee cup.

"Sounds as if you've had a busy day. I'd better not hold you up any longer." I wish this awkwardness would disappear.

He gives a nod goodbye and takes a step away then hesitates. "What're you doing tonight?"

His question catches me off-guard and I struggle to find any words.

"She has nothing on tonight," Lily chimes in with a smile, kicking me under the table.

I subtly raise my eyes at Lily as if to say *what are you doing?* I quickly turn back to Sam and try to think of an excuse for whatever it is he is about to ask. "We're moving on Sunday, so I'm still packing, sorry."

"Oh, that's a shame." He honestly sounds a little defeated. "I'm having a small get-together tonight for my birthday, but since I've only been here a little while, I don't really have a lot of friends to invite. Would have been nice to have you there. Both of you if you wanted. Especially seeing as you're leaving soon."

And now I feel guilty. I thought he was trying to ask me out on a date, but he was just looking for a friend.

Lily kicks me again under the table. "I already have plans tonight, but I'm sure Kaylee could spare an hour or so to go."

Both are staring at me, waiting for my response. I've never been good with letting people down and I finally give in. "You know what? I could do with a couple of hours off. But I'll have to get back home pretty early to keep packing so won't be able to stay long." I add the last bit to allow myself an early exit if the night goes south.

Sam gives me a large smile. "Perfect. Here, what's your number? I'll text you the details."

He passes me his phone and I add my contact details. It quickly crosses my mind to put the number in wrong to get me out of tonight, but maybe I was right. I have been packing and training nonstop, so I could do with an hour or so off.

"Great, well I'll see you tonight." He walks away with a bounce in his step.

When he's out of sight I death stare Lily.

"What? He's cute, you're single, and it was obvious he had a thing for you that night at the club. What's the harm?"

It takes all my energy to hold in my frustration. "We're about to move."

"Well, you have nothing to lose then, so use it as practice on how to get a guy for the next town."

I groan. I don't know whether she's hoping I'll fall for someone and change my mind on joining Headquarters, or if she's just trying to get me to move on from Vincent, but either way I don't have the patience for this conversation. I quickly finish off my smoothie and motion to the exit.

She seems to smile in satisfaction but follows my lead and drives me home.

By the time we arrive I've already received the details from Sam. Lily informs me that the address is just a few streets from where we live, which is handy.

"Are you sure you won't come tonight?" I ask her.

She shifts in her seat. "I'm already meeting some friends tonight."

I give her a questioning look as we exit the car and she just shrugs. No further details are provided. I'm too caught up in figuring out what I'm going to wear tonight, and where I've packed all my good clothes, to worry about her plans so I don't bother asking for more details.

As expected, it ends up taking me a good hour to find everything I need to go out tonight, then another hour and a half to assemble myself.

With a few spare minutes before I need to leave, I have time to think about what I'm doing. I'm going over to visit someone I hardly know, to spend time with a bunch of strangers that I don't know at all. Why am I doing this? I pick up my phone and try to come up with reasons on why I can't go tonight but each excuse is obvious. I already told him I couldn't stay long, so surely, I can do this for an hour?

I drag myself downstairs before I talk myself out of going and let Aunt Amy know I'm leaving, promising her I'll be home before nine. I can't find Lily, so I suspect she's already left for the night.

I pull up to the curb in front of a tidy two-story house and notice there's only two other cars here. I contemplate sitting in the car a while longer to wait for more people to turn up, but Sam emerges from the front door and waves toward me. I take a deep breath and go out to greet him.

"Thanks for coming!" he says as I get closer.

"It's good to be out of the house," I reply awkwardly.

"Come on in." He opens the front door, and luckily everything inside is bright and welcoming. I have only met Sam three times so I can't be too cautious.

He leads me through the house, mentioning off the rooms as we go. "And this is the entertainment room."

I walk into a large room that has a pool table off to one side and long couches facing a wide screen TV on the opposite side. Music is playing in the background and there's someone on the couch with some sort of console remote in her hands.

He introduces me to Kiera, who is the splitting image of Sam in a female version. She's not overweight, but has a solid build like him, with the same square jawline and jet-black hair. They must be siblings, or close cousins as they seem to be around the same age.

"Oh, happy birthday by the way," I say, when I remember.

"Thanks. There should be some work friends coming soon too, but that's about as crazy as tonight will get." There's an odd tone to his voice. Maybe he's disheartened that he doesn't have more friends coming tonight?

Kiera holds out the gaming remote to me. "Want to play?"

I hold back a blush. "Ah, I don't really know how."

Sam and Kiera exchange glances and laugh. "That's fine. I'll show you," she replies.

She introduces me to Tekken and asks me to pick out a character. As I scroll through people of different shapes, sizes, and nationalities I stop on a character named Katarina. Her chest is so voluptuous that I'm surprised it's not protruding from the TV.

Kiera puts me in training mode and shows me how to do different combinations with my character, all the while making light conversation about my upbringing, where we're moving to and my family dynamic. It starts to feel as if I'm meeting a boyfriend's family.

"What do you like to do in your spare time?" she asks.

Besides martial arts and having a supernatural gift? "I like to go hiking." Technically there's a little bit of hiking involved when I go out to Pop's.

"Oh, that's pretty exciting. Where do you go?"

"Just out in the forest," I reply vaguely.

Sam returns with some nibbles and puts them on the coffee table. "Would you like a drink?"

"Oh, I've got to drive so can't drink, but thanks."

"Seeing you're underage it wouldn't be right of me to give you an alcoholic drink." He gives me a wink and we both laugh. "We've got soft drinks or juice as well though."

"Some juice would be nice, thanks."

He returns shortly after and we all continue playing Tekken, taking it in turns to verse each other even though I lose every time. I'm about to start another round of fighting when my vision starts to go fuzzy. I turn to Kiera and try to speak, but the words come out slurred. Something is not right. I attempt to stand up, but my legs give way and the room spins as I fall.

Sam grabs onto my shoulders and helps lower me to the ground. "It's easier if you don't fight it."

I stare up at him with wide eyes in horror, then my vision goes black.

CHAPTER NINETEEN

My eyelids blink heavily, and I struggle to bring clarity to my vision. I let out an involuntary groan, and in the process a discomfort in my jaw awakens my senses. As I move my mouth, my teeth bite down on something foreign. I try to lift my hands up to pull it away, but a sharp pain radiates through my wrists which refuse to budge from behind my back. My heart begins to race as panic sets in. I shake my body, trying to move anything, but I'm tightly secured to a chair.

"You're finally awake." A male voice speaks, and I turn my head to see Sam. Gone are his kind eyes and happy smile, and instead, his face is empty of all emotion. I'd always felt at ease around him, but as his tall, strong body towers over mine, I'm terrified. What is he doing? What does he want from me? Is he going to hurt me? So many questions quickly run through my mind. If the past few weeks have taught me anything, it's to not allow my emotions to overcome me. It takes every ounce of strength to remain in control. Right now, my life could depend on it.

I try to speak, but my voice is muffled against the restraint around my mouth.

"You're just going to sit there and listen first, okay?"

I can't talk, so I slowly nod. The more time he's talking, the more time I have to figure out what to do.

"There is someone that we're looking for, and I know that you know where he is. If you tell me his location, we'll let you go. It's as simple as that."

Who could he possibly be after?

"Where's Vincent's grandfather?"

Pop? I attempt to hide the shock on my face but I'm not sure if I'm doing a good job. I try to talk, knowing it's going to be muffled, but hoping he understands my intentions.

He recognizes what I'm trying to do because he gives me a warning. "Scream and we will knock you out."

I nod in reply, then realize he's said *we*. Kiera must be around. That complicates matters.

He removes the material from around my mouth and I stretch my jaw to bring some relief. I quickly pull myself together and try to put on my best performance. "I'd only known Vincent for that one week when we met, Sam, and the only family of his that I met was his brother. I didn't even know he had a grandfather who lived around here. You know Vincent moved away, so maybe his family is gone too?"

He shakes his head and makes a repetitive *tsk* sound. "We'd spent so long trying to figure out if the grandfather was attached to anyone. It's not often your kind leaves one of your own to fend for themselves. Initially, we could only track him by the short visits Vincent and Tyler made every few months. Then I met you..." He takes a small pause, as if to let his words sink in. "We'd always hoped that I'd gain some information from working with Vincent, but you were the missing piece we'd been waiting for. That first night we met in the club was a lovely show that you put on. I mean, Vincent did a good job covering it up, but I'd known what you were as soon as I saw you. You truly are a reflection of your mother." As he speaks my stomach ties in knots. Tracking. My mother. This is XET. "And it turns out that when we plot your history in the last few years, it so happens to match up nicely to where Vincent and Tyler have visited often."

I try to say something. Anything. But my mouth is utterly dry. All this time everyone had warned me that I needed to get my skills under control, so I didn't lead XET to us, but I've done exactly that. Another clue from his tirade sticks out. They've been watching Vincent and Tyler for a while now but haven't attacked them. Why? And he hasn't made a move yet against me. He just wants information about Pop. Why Pop? I know I need to stall them to try work out how to get out of this uninjured, but I can also try and find out anything I can. There's no point trying to deny what I am. They obviously know more than possibly even I do.

I stare Sam directly in the eyes. "Sam, I promise you that I only just found out about this life a few weeks ago, which is why the accident occurred at the club. I was having a panic attack and it just escaped from me." This sparks another thought. "I don't want to hurt you, but I can't control myself yet. It would be best for your safety if you would untie me and we can talk about this in a less intimidating manner, so I don't have another panic attack."

He briefly pauses then walks away. I hear an altercation between Sam and I'm presuming Kiera, but she stops talking and he walks back into view.

I'd never imagined what it would be like to be face-to-face with my death, but as I stare down the barrel of a gun, I freeze. My stomach threatens to bring up the day's contents, and I'm faint again, feeling all color drain from my face.

"Let me make this very clear. You are here to serve a purpose, and that is to disclose the location of Vincent's grandfather. If you cannot fulfill this purpose, then I have no use for you. Got it?"

I quickly nod. There is no stalling anymore. This means right now I must decide whose life is more important. Mine or Pop's.

"And before you get any ideas, Kiera will be checking the location before we release you, so don't send us to the wrong address."

My head scrambles to decide. Every human has an innate sense of self preservation, but I would be knowingly sending someone to their death. Sam hasn't dropped the gun and as I continue to stare at it my breath becomes shallower and I choke on the lump at the back of my throat. *I'm not ready to die.* The thought causes my eyes to fill with tears and they begin to escape down the sides of my face. My body begins to shake, and I struggle to breathe as a panic attack settles in. I can't give them Pop's location.

"Sam..." I plead, "please... I don't want to die."

Sam pulls back on the gun and it clicks into position. His face is unmoving. I let out a sob, and gasp as I try to inhale. The temperature in the room feels as if it's dropped and the air hangs thick around me. It's as though he has a hand around my throat, and I can't get enough oxygen in.

The thought sets off an image in my head from weeks ago. A moment with Mom where Vincent was grasping at his throat because he couldn't breathe. Mom had done that to him. She'd manipulated the air out of his lungs. Could I do that? Right now, I'm out of options so I have to try. To make matters worse, my hands are behind my back, but I have no choice but to figure out a way to achieve it without them.

I can't let Sam know I'm trying to fool him.

"Okay!" I scream. The effects of the once-looming panic attack are still evident on my body and I try to keep them going. Sam must think I'm panicking. "I'll... tell you... where he is," I say between gasps, "just please... put down the gun... I can't breathe. I can't breathe."

He cocks his head to the side, as if he's deciding whether I'm trustworthy or not, and then he lowers the gun.

I let out an honest sigh of relief. If I'm going to try something, it will be better if the gun isn't pointed at me, in case he cues in on to what's happening. I make an act of taking multiple deep breaths as if to calm myself, but instead I take the opportunity to regenerate and focus my mind.

From the beginning, I've always had a good grasp on my element. As soon as I began training with it, I could sense the air vibrating around me. But where do I even begin on trying to shift it out of his lungs? When I make whirlwinds, I focus on grabbing threads of air and redirecting it to where I want it, but I don't have wind to work with or the use of my hands.

I analyze his breathing, the air around him shifting in and out of his body. I sense it vibrating around his face, watching the flow. If I'd had my hands free, I would have reached forward and grabbed at the threads of air in front of his mouth, but now all I have is my mind. As he lets out another exhale, I visualize what I want to achieve, hoping to will it into action. I send imaginary hands forward and tug a little more on the thread of air that is expelled on his breath out, causing slightly more air to come out of his lungs than he intended.

Sam raises his eyebrows at me, waiting for me to continue. I need to multi-task. "It's hard to tell you where he lives because it's not an actual address," I begin, watching him closely. "He lives out in the forest just south of Asheville. To be honest it might be easier for me to take you there instead of trying to give directions."

"Just give me the location," Sam says, taking a deep

breath after he speaks. His chest moves up and down rapidly, as though he's having a hard time breathing.

I send my imaginary hands forward again and again, pulling ever so slightly at each breath. I use only minimal movements to not give me away, but to prove if it's working.

He takes another deep breath, this time slightly longer.

Is it working? I can't take any more chances. It's now or never.

I concentrate everything I have on the air surrounding his face and with his next exhale, I yank as hard as I can with my imaginary hands, withdrawing the majority of the air that remains inside his lungs. His chest rises as he attempts to refill his lungs, but I mentally hold firm on the air around him, not allowing a thread to return. He opens his mouth wide, but still no air returns. His eyes shut as his face crumples in despair. He reaches one hand to his throat and clutches it so tightly he wouldn't be able to breathe if I let the air back in. The other hand begins to rise, shaking as if it's taking all his energy to aim. The gun is almost at chest level and I try and shift myself in the chair, away from the firing line. I know the outcome will be decided in the next few seconds.

His finger budges against the trigger.

My heart beats so hard it reverberates throughout my body.

His legs wobble and the gun loses aim.

I take a sharp inhale, readying for my fate.

His body slumps to the floor.

I almost let out a cry of relief until I hear a voice call out.

"Sam?"

KIERA!

As she comes into view, I jump straight into action, trying to remove her oxygen, but it's difficult to focus on two people at once and my energy is dwindling. Beads of sweat begin to run down my forehead.

She makes a move for the gun.

"He's just sleeping!" I scream at her. "Please you don't want to do this, he's going to be okay if you let me go." I'm almost crying.

I know as soon as she pulls that trigger the air will immediately return to Sam and he will be fine, but she doesn't know that.

My comment makes her pause.

I focus on the air around her and again withdraw as she exhales, but it's not even enough to make her inhale deeply with the following breath and my head starts to spin as my energy wavers. I can't do it. But I don't have any other choice, so I continue to focus on the air around her, willing to fight to the death. She takes a long deep breath and looks to Sam, then to me, confused. I can tell she's putting the pieces together. My vision starts speckling as I reach empty. My efforts haven't been enough. She takes the final step toward the gun. I hope her aim is true to finish this as quickly and painlessly as possible.

I close my eyes and a single tear runs down my cheek as a loud sound echoes through the room, my body jolting in response.

But nothing eventuates.

Another loud crash shocks me enough to open my eyes and Kiera's pressed up against the wall, the pool table pinning her in place. I follow the movement to my left and the tears flow as I take in all of Vincent. His face is plastered with rage, but it quickly softens when he sees me, and that I'm okay. He rushes over to me and works on my bindings as Tyler and Lily follow and both set to work on securing Sam and Kiera. A bubble of water appears in front of Kiera's face as Tyler talks to her. She nods and remains still as he pushes the pool table off her. She doubles over, clutching her ribs, but makes no other attempt at moving as Tyler ties her up. Sam on the other hand is still passed out even though I've lost focus on the air around him. Lily has tied him up anyway. It won't be long before he wakes.

In the same time it takes for Lily and Tyler to act, Vincent has my bindings undone. An ache courses through my shoulders as my arms are finally released.

I stand on unsteady legs, but Vincent is there to support me. I reach up to his face, needing to touch it to make sure what I'm seeing is real.

He presses his face into my hand and a gut-wrenching sob escapes as I wrap my arms around him and nuzzle my face into his neck, his scent coursing through my body. The tears flow relentlessly, and he gently holds onto me as I let everything out.

He's really here!

The next few minutes pass in a blur. I walk about mindlessly as everyone moves around me. My brain is unable to formulate a single thought.

Lily parks her car in the garage and Vincent and Tyler assist Sam and Kiera into the back seat. They discuss where to go, but the only option is to take them to the cellar out at Pop's.

I finally chime in about Sam wanting Pop's location. They all look at me with worry. Vincent, Tyler, and Lily discuss the complications surrounding taking XET to their target, and they all agree that Pop has to stay away from the cellar. They'll take whatever means necessary to keep him away from XET.

My attention piques as they begin to deliberate who's taking me home.

Vincent's eyes pierce me with the same longing that I've been holding onto for weeks. "I should really help Tyler with these two," he says to Lily, motioning to the back of the car. "In case they get any ideas."

Lily rolls her eyes. "Don't be stupid. Take Kaylee home. Plus, I think you forget who won our last fight." She adds the last bit in with a smirk.

Lily gives me a small smile and nods, as if accepting this new dynamic.

Vincent rubs the back of his neck, obviously conflicted, but Lily orders, "Go! She needs to get to bed."

I didn't even realize I was yawning, but the adrenaline of the night seems to have subsided, and my body feels full of lead.

Vincent turns to Tyler and Lily. "I'll meet you there tomorrow. The first sign of resistance, don't hesitate." He passes the gun to Tyler who pauses for a second before reaching out to take it.

Vincent waits until they've left, and then he turns his attention back to me. By now I've slumped myself against a wall, too exhausted to keep upright.

"Oh, Kaylee." He looks at me sympathetically and picks me up, taking me to Aunt Amy's car.

I don't remember falling asleep, but the next time I open my eyes I'm being carried out of the car. Vincent knocks on the door with what I presume to be his foot, so he doesn't have to put me down. Aunt Amy answers and begins to panic.

"She's okay," Vincent reassures her. "I'll put her to bed and then fill you in."

Aunt Amy reaches out and strokes the side of my cheek, worry across her face. She obviously wants more information, but she steps aside and takes Vincent to my room.

He lays me down and I reach out for his hand, not wanting him to leave.

"I'll be right back," he assures me.

The frown reappears on Aunt Amy, but she doesn't say anything. I'll leave that conversation between the two of them.

They don't even make it to the door before my eyes close.

CHAPTER TWENTY

I'm woken by strong, warm arms wrapping around me. I roll toward him and curl myself into his chest as he presses his lips against the top of my head. His chest rises and falls and soon we are synchronized, our bodies together, our chests moving in harmony as if we are one. He plants a final gentle kiss on my forehead, and I close my eyes and quickly resettle back to sleep.

My dreams twist to and fro from nightmares to good dreams. I dream of Vincent, then I dream of XET. I wake up numerous times calling out for help, but every time he pulls me in to him, shielding me from the world around us. I let him take me away from my thoughts, my concerns, and my fears. I absorb myself in his scent and lay my hand against his heart, feeling it beat and letting the rhythm lull me back to sleep.

When morning arrives, Vincent's kneeling by the side of the bed. I stare at him for some time, gazing into the depths of his eyes, making sure he's truly here. Suddenly the memories of last night flood through my mind and I can't stop my face from scrunching up in pain. Vincent presses his forehead into mine, wrapping his arm around me. I have never been so scared in my life. I did everything I could, but it still wasn't enough.

But Vincent came for me.

"How did you know what was happening?" I finally ask.

"Tyler and I had returned to help Pop move as it takes a lot of effort to demolish the old house and recreate the new cabin. Lily had just picked us up from the airport and Tyler asked about you. She said you were with Sam for his birthday and I immediately knew something was wrong." He gently runs his hand along the frown on my forehead.

How did he know something was wrong?

He answers my unspoken question. "When I took Sam on, I had a copy of his driver's license and his birthday stood out to me as it was the same as Pop's, which isn't for another three months."

Sam had obviously needed to figure out a way to get me alone, and he played on my guilt by saying he didn't have many coming for a birthday get-together. I fell straight into his trap.

"Lily remembered the street name that you'd said, and we saw Amy's car parked out front. Everything seemed fine until we got to the front door. It was too quiet. I broke down the door, and when I saw her turning the gun toward you..." He buries his head into the mattress. He looks back up at me with glistening eyes and places a gentle hand against my cheek. "I'm sorry I wasn't here to protect you. I was the one who introduced you to Sam. I don't know how I missed it."

I try to find the words to tell him it's not his fault, but his first statement sticks in my head. He wasn't here. And he's going to leave again. I'm so overwhelmed by the pain of last night, and now I need to face losing Vincent again.

"Why are you here, Vincent?" I ask softly. My body shudders with pain as the question escapes. Why do I constantly sabotage us?

"I told you, to help Pop move." He looks at me, confused.

"No. Why are you here, in my room? Lily could have taken me home."

His face drops. "Don't you want me here?"

"Of course I do! But that's the problem because you're just going to leave me again." My voice catches and I struggle to hide the pain from him.

He moves back from the bed and I sit up, readying myself for this conversation.

"You were the one who pushed me away. Remember?" The pain is evident in his voice.

"For this exact reason. You want to just come in and out of my life, but it hurts. It hurts so much. I miss you beyond words when you're gone, and I'm in constant agony when you're here because I know you're going to leave again." I can't hold it in anymore. If I give him the truth, all of it, then he can decide what he does with the facts.

He opens his mouth to speak but no words come out.

I need to get out of this room. Everything is so suffocating.

"Where are you going?" he calls after me.

"To have a shower."

I stand under the water for minutes as my mind runs wild with memories of last night and my argument with Vincent. Why am I doing this? Wasn't I just devastated that he wasn't here? And now he is, I'm ruining it. I never want to go through the pain of losing him again, so we need to have this conversation. Right now, I can't take any more painful thoughts, so I force my mind to wander to something happy. The sound of the water reminds me of the waterfall at the plateau. I think about the time we were lying on the bank of the stream and Vincent was beside me whispering that he wasn't a bad person. Then he leaned over and our lips touched. I remember feeling as if the world stopped and in that one moment the only thing that mattered was the connection between the two of us. The spark lights just thinking about it and I touch my lips, remembering the feeling.

There is no pain in this memory. Just pure lust between two people, connecting in an unimaginable way.

I open my eyes and my breathing is heavy. I shake my head to clear my mind, because these thoughts only lead to pain, but it's stuck on Vincent. It's constantly stuck on Vincent. This boy has a hold of my heart and I don't know how to let that go.

I finish showering and wrap the towel around me. As I open the door, there's someone standing in the doorway. My heart skips a beat and I thrust my fist forward but stop myself an inch short of his nose. Vincent stands before me, looking at my fist. I let my arm drop and take a deep breath. He reaches for me and pulls me into his arms.

"I'm sorry, Kaylee, I didn't mean to scare you."

I settle my breathing, but it only lasts a few seconds before I realize I'm standing there only wearing a towel. My heart races faster and I know he can probably feel it. I look up into his eyes and see the same longing that I so desperately feel.

His hand skims my bare back, moving my wet hair over my shoulder, and it is my undoing. I reach up and press my lips against his. The electricity is immediate and radiates throughout my whole body. Just once I want this. A kiss without over-thinking, without hesitation, without any uncertainty whatsoever. His hands hold me gently, allowing me to make any moves.

I don't know what I would do if I couldn't do this with him.

A tear rolls down my cheek. He pulls back and wipes away the tear, holding on to the side of my face. He places his lips against my forehead and squeezes me tight.

I give Vincent the truth again. "I love you so much that it hurts, and I'm so scared I'm going to lose you because that would destroy me." He has my heart. All of it. I'm scared he won't want it, or that he'll leave for XET and find someone else, or that something will happen to him with XET.

"Kaylee," he whispers and pulls me into his chest again. "I love you too."

He loves me too? Within the tears I let out a happy laugh which comes out more like a snort, and then I smile. I look up at him and he responds with the most heartfelt smile that reaches into the depths of his eyes and it catches my breath.

"So, what now?" I ask, desperate for him to have the answers.

"I don't know what's going to happen in the future, but here, today, I choose you."

Those three simple words resonate within me. I choose him too. I must find a way to be happy with that answer and deal with each day as they come because sacrificing what we have because of what-ifs isn't making either of us happy. I reach up and kiss him again then quickly remember my current state of clothing.

I blush. "I need to get dressed."

He gives me a look which says otherwise, and the heat radiates in my cheeks. I quickly walk away.

When I finally emerge, Vincent is standing in the doorway rubbing his neck. "I need to leave."

I look at him with wide eyes. "Are you serious?"

"I have to go to Pop's to figure out what's happening with

the two hostages," he elaborates, "but I'll come back once it's all sorted."

"No!" I stamp my foot. "Don't treat me like a child. I'm coming too."

He says something in protest, but I refuse to budge. "This is not negotiable."

He hesitates, but nods.

A nauseating wave flows through my body. Am I ready to see the two people who held a gun to me last night? If I still plan on joining Headquarters, then I need to pull myself together. This is part of the job. My hands shake, defying the confidence in my mind.

———

TYLER MEETS US OUTSIDE AS SOON AS WE ARRIVE. NOT THAT there's much to catch up on. Sam and Kiera are being kept in separate cells and the only thing they're saying is that they want to talk to the grandfather alone.

There it is again. All they want is Pop. What is it that they want from him?

Lily and Tyler have outright refused to let him be alone with them. Lily has threatened to light the cellar on fire if he attempts to try. They both took turns staying down there all night to ensure Pop has never been alone with them, and to try and pick up on any clues in case Sam and Kiera talk to each other.

"So, what's the whole point of keeping them captive?" I ask.

Vincent answers, "We try to get any information out of them regarding their plans. Current targets, locations, end goal." He pauses. "And once we're finished, we are to dispose of them."

I take a step back. Dispose? He makes it sound as though he's dealing with a bag of garbage. These are human beings.

"What do you want us to do with them, Kaylee?" he asks me, looking as though he genuinely wants me to give a better solution.

I shake my head. "I don't know. But surely that isn't the answer."

Tyler finally pipes up. "If we let them go, we may as well point a gun at one another and pull the trigger. Because the first chance they get, they'll be doing exactly that."

"But they didn't pull the trigger. All they wanted to know from me was where Pop lived." I don't know why I'm defending them. They both held a gun to me and as far as I was aware, both were willing to pull that trigger if I didn't oblige. "If they're willing to talk to Pop, what harm could that do? They're still locked up and secluded from the outside world. And then maybe you'll get some of your answers about their goals."

"What harm? We've led them straight to the person they want. These people are cunning, and they obviously have a plan. It is in our best interests to get in the way of whatever it is they want, even if it seems harmless," Vincent replies.

I don't want to fight with him. Not after today.

Vincent says firmly, "We use today to get what we can out of them, and to pack this place down. We leave at first light back to Kaylee's then start the journey to Wisconsin. Got it?"

I nod in agreement, but I know this can't be the solution.

As we make our way inside, Pop is waiting in the living room. He's livid.

"Please tell me the two of you aren't as stupid as this lot?" He looks at Vincent and me for an answer. Obviously, he doesn't agree with the existing plan either. I look down at the floor, trying to avoid eye contact.

Vincent answers his question. "You call them the stupid ones when you're wanting to give XET exactly what they want?"

"I'd be in my right mind to toss the lot of you out right now and be done with this all," Pop replies, pacing back and forth.

"Go ahead, but you'll be left with fried captives." Vincent replies firmly. Then his tone softens. "You are the only family we have left. You're not going down there alone."

It seems to be the comment Pop needed. He opens his mouth to talk but sits back down, his face still furrowed with anger.

I'd wondered why he was so against Pop going down, but perhaps it's not just to do with giving XET what they want, but more the fact he doesn't want Pop being put in danger. He's already lost his parents to XET, and I don't think he's forgiven himself for their death.

Vincent makes his way down to the cellar and I follow. He turns around when he hears my footsteps. "Perhaps it's best if you leave XET to the rest of us?" His eyes are pleading, but I know he won't deny me if I object.

I don't think I've taken the time yet to process what happened last night. It was so surreal that it feels as though it could have been a dream. Can I even face the two of them, knowing what is in store for them tomorrow morning? If there's any way of getting out of that option then I need to take the chance, so until that moment, I decide it's best I'm involved as much as possible.

"No, I'm fine." It takes all my effort to try to hide my hesitation. We make our way down the dark stairwell, and I concentrate on keeping my shaking hands steady.

I don't know what I was expecting to find, but the calm picture in front of me–Lily sitting, reading a magazine, and the two captives lying on their beds staring up at the roof–is not what I had envisioned.

"Tag, you're it," she says unenthusiastically and makes her way upstairs. She doesn't look either of us in the eyes and although she offered for Vincent to take me home yesterday, it's going to take her some time to adjust to the two of us.

Sam finally looks up to see who's arrived and smiles.

"Well played." He looks at me, grinning.

I look over at Sam and a flashback of him holding the gun to my head runs through my mind. I almost double over to vomit. Well played? Because my life is a game? The anger boils inside me. "This isn't a game Sam. You held a gun to my head last night. Does that even register with you? Do you even care? What sort of person does that?" It pours out of me as my brain struggles to hold onto one thought.

He chuckles. "Take a look around, Kaylee. It seems you know exactly what sort of person it takes to do that."

"You put me in this position!" My voice is rising even though Sam is speaking calmly.

Vincent finally steps in between the two of us, grabbing onto my hand. His physical presence helps to calm my heart and mind.

He addresses Sam. "Tell us what you want with my grandfather."

"Bring him down here and leave us alone, then he can fill you in on what we're after," Sam replies smugly.

Suddenly the floor rumbles and a rectangular barrier encases Kiera's bed from floor to ceiling. A muffled scream penetrates through. "How long do you think it'll take for her to run out of air in there, Sam? Your gamble. You know how this ends for the two of you, so just give us what we want and let's not drag this out."

My heart starts galloping. This wasn't supposed to

happen. Sam lies back down on the table. "If you're not going to let us talk to your grandfather, then you may as well kill us both now."

"Your choice." Vincent walks back upstairs, leaving the box around Kiera. Sam doesn't flinch.

As soon as we emerge upstairs, I press myself against the hallway, taking in a deep breath. I hadn't realized how claustrophobic I had felt down there until I emerged into the cool fresh air.

"Hey, I'm here, okay?" Vincent reassures me while gently grabbing onto my wrists.

I nod. Perhaps I'm not ready for this.

Vincent asks Tyler to take over the watch downstairs, and then addresses me. "We need to start getting everything in motion to move tomorrow morning. I've got to go and grab my pickup to load everything into. Come with me?"

I don't know why I don't want to go, but a gnawing feeling telling me that I have to stay settles in my mind. "I might stay and help pack."

Vincent hesitates but doesn't object. "Okay. I'll be back as soon as I can." He kisses me on the forehead and leaves.

CHAPTER TWENTY-ONE

Nothing about this situation sits right with me. Near death experience. Captives. Torture. But for some reason I can't stay away.

I look around the house and find Pop in the kitchen packing. With nothing else to do, I join him to help. We work in silence, neither really knowing what to say.

He suddenly stops moving and looks around us before addressing me. "You know I need to get down there and talk to them."

I don't respond, just continue packing. I don't know why, but I feel the same way. Perhaps that's why I stayed. But Vincent would never forgive me.

"If there's anything that I can do that might protect the rest of you, then isn't that worth the risk?" he implores further.

This was precisely what Vincent didn't want. Him putting his life on the line for the rest of us.

I can't stand listening to him plead with me, but I can't face telling him no. I put the jar I'm holding back on the bench, and I walk away. Did he try this on Lily or Tyler?

I decide it's best to move to another room, and I am drawn to Vincent's. The door is shut and when I open it Lily is fast asleep on his bed. I softly shut the door again.

A nagging voice emerges in my mind saying there's only one more person in the way of getting Pop downstairs and I quickly try and shove the thought aside.

I pace back and forward down the hallway, contemplating. Maybe if I'm alone with Sam I can get more information? My stomach tenses at the thought of having to face him. He seems to talk when I'm down there though. I let that excuse convince me into going back downstairs.

Tyler's sitting in the chair with his head rolled back. He and Lily have been taking turns all night to watch the two of them, and he must be exhausted.

"Why don't you go and have a rest?" My voice sounds strange and I'm waiting for him to jump up and tell me he can see right through my facade, but instead he gives me a thankful look and leaves me alone.

My heart races. Everything has fallen into place too easily.

I look over at Sam and swallow my emotions. It's an odd mixture; fear, guilt, and anger. It doesn't sit well in my stomach.

I get straight to the point. Who knows how much time I have? "Why is Vincent's grandfather so important?"

He turns his head to me and smiles. "If we don't talk to him now, we will not stop chasing him. You're only holding off the inevitable. Or you can let us see him, alone, and we'll stop. Stop chasing him and leave you, and your friends, alone."

He said that yesterday; that if I gave him what he wanted he'd let me go. Now he's promising to back off all of us. It seems too good to be true. But what else could he be playing at while he's locked away?

A firm hand rests on my shoulders and I jump at the contact. I turn around to Pop staring at me with tired eyes. "It's okay, child. This is my choice. Let me play my part."

Sam sits up at Pop's voice, watching us expectantly.

Everything is screaming at me to tell Pop to go away, but at the same time, knowledge is power. And if there's any truth to Sam's promise of safety, then I need to take it. They're locked away, so what is there to lose?

Swallowing back my betrayal of Vincent, I turn around and walk up the stairs, giving XET exactly what they wanted.

Time seems to slow down as soon as I shut the door. My heart is pounding in my ears so even if they were talking loud enough to hear, I wouldn't be able to. I'm expecting Lily or Tyler to walk out any second and see how I've deceived them. But no one comes. And the door behind me opens sooner than I anticipated.

Pop shrugs. "Waste of time. Nothing we didn't already know."

He walks to the kitchen and continues packing as if nothing even happened.

"Well, what did they say?" I pry further. I didn't just betray Vincent's trust to be left out of the loop.

"It turns out that I killed their mother eight years ago."

So they are siblings! I can't think further on it as Pop continues.

"They've been on a side project ever since to try and find me. He had some words for his mother's killer. From what I can gather, XET don't even know they're here. That's why they've promised everyone's safety because they're only after me."

A lump forms in my throat. "So, what do we do now?"

"They're our captives and we'll be dealing with them in the morning. Problem solved." He starts packing again.

As much as I hate Sam and Kiera, I do feel sorrow for them. Because of us, they lost their mother. There's been so much pain and killing on both sides by the looks of it. Where does it end?

And I have less than one day to come to terms with being an accomplice to murder. Because that's what it will be. The fact I know about it and do nothing, makes me just as much a part of the killing.

The thought makes me nauseous, but no one is down there with Sam and Kiera, and if I don't go back down, Tyler or Lily will know something has happened. No one needs to find out what we know yet. It doesn't make a difference.

I quietly make my way back downstairs and take a seat. Sam gives me a nod and I respond in same. I can't imagine what it would be like to be face-to-face with the person that killed someone you loved, but I hope having that chance to express himself gives him some closure.

I do notice, however, that the flow of air has changed around the wall containing Kiera. I focus closer and can sense air exchanging at the top of the back wall, completely out of sight. Will Vincent be able to tell his wall has been broken and know it was Pop? Is it worth risking Vincent finding out when they're going to be dealt with anyway tomorrow? There's nothing that I can do to repair the wall and I can't stomach being involved with torturing her more, so I let it go.

Sam doesn't say another word, just lies on the bed staring at the roof. It seems he's now content, having had his time with Pop.

I lose track of time, but eventually Lily comes to relieve me. I head back upstairs and pass the time by helping to pack up. Not long after, the sound of an engine grows closer and

Vincent emerges from his pickup. Lily's car is no longer in the driveway so he must have swapped cars.

He gives me a hug and a pang of guilt courses through me. I resign myself to the fact that I will divulge the truth. But not today; there's enough going on and it doesn't change our plan.

Vincent makes his way inside and heads for the cellar door. What if Sam tells him I've let Pop down there!

"Lily just woke up and has taken over." I quickly try to distract him. "Why don't we pack up your room since it's free?"

He gives me a nod and I let out a sigh of relief. I've avoided that conversation, for now.

I help as much as possible to pack up his room and I skim my hand over the photo frame once I get to the bedside table.

"Your mother was beautiful."

"She was that and more." There's a haunting sorrow to his voice. "She was fierce, protective and smart. And so loving."

"Did you join Headquarters for revenge?" I ask. My thoughts have drifted to Sam who also lost his mother.

"No!" he quickly responds. "Although it does make it easier when we're faced with tough decisions–like Sam and Kiera–knowing what their kind have taken away from me. I wanted to help Headquarters because I'm sick of living with a target on my back. Can you imagine what it would feel like to be able to live somewhere, knowing you'd never have to leave?"

I sigh. I wish that so much.

"Where does this end?" I ask desperately. "XET chase us, we retaliate against them. How much more death does there need to be?"

"As much as it takes for them to leave us alone. We're not the bad people here. If XET weren't after us, then we wouldn't be chasing them. The cycle begins and ends with them."

"Surely we can get them to back off without killing them?"

Vincent throws his hands up. "What would you have us do? Go up to them and say, *You know it'd be really nice if you'd stop chasing us. Thanks*? Want to go down there and see how well that works with Sam? Because I'm not willing to risk your life on niceties."

I don't know how to respond. I don't have any other solution.

We're interrupted by footsteps down the hallway. Tyler's woken from his nap.

Vincent looks at me. "If Lily has only just taken over, and Tyler was sleeping, who was watching Sam and Kiera?"

"I was," I reply matter-of-factly, trying to remain calm.

"Tyler!" Vincent calls out.

"Stop treating me like a child, Vincent," I rebut firmly.

"What did they say to you? Did they try anything?" His eyes penetrate me, hungry for answers.

"They didn't say anything. Well if Kiera did, I couldn't hear her anyway." I give him a big eye roll.

Her name seems to remind him about her circumstances and he quickly makes his way to the cellar. Tyler sluggishly moves out of the way, having been standing in the doorway since Vincent called him, shrugs at me, then continues to the bathroom. He could really do with more sleep.

I follow Vincent anxiously as I wait for Sam to reveal the truth.

"Are you ready to talk yet, or shall I keep Kiera enclosed? I mean, I can't guarantee that she's even still breathing."

Sam looks to me with a grin. He knows I haven't told Vincent.

"Maybe she might be more cooperative?" Vincent mistakes his smile as insolence.

A wave of dust washes through the room as a wall erupts around Sam and the one around Kiera drops.

She's flushed and covered in sweat. While she might have been given a breathing hole, the heat would have been another factor to combat.

"I will kill you," she says with a look of fury on her face, directed at Vincent.

Vincent raises his eyebrows as he looks at me, as if to prove his point of our earlier discussion.

"Go ahead," Vincent tries her. "But in the meantime, Sam's suffocating. So, if you'd rather waste your time hating me, rather than working with me, then that's your choice."

She looks over to Sam's cellar and she at least has the decency to look worried, unlike his reaction when the roles were reversed. I'm not sure if she knows that Sam has spoken to Pop.

"I'll be back in an hour. See if you're ready to talk then." He turns around and storms back up the stairs.

Kiera sits on the edge of the bed rubbing her hands across her forehead. She looks terrible. She sways then races to the toilet and vomits. Have they even had any water while they've been down here?

I grab some water from the kitchen and place it inside Kiera's cell. She stares at it, unmoving.

"It's not poisoned," I assure her.

She moves closer and grabs the glass, taking a small sip initially, then guzzles the whole drink with a satisfied sigh at the end.

"Thank you," she says, surprising me.

She gets up off the floor and slumps onto the bed. I don't think she'll be in any mood to talk in an hour, let alone the rest of the afternoon. She had only been enclosed for about three hours, so I'll have to put a word in to Pop to create another air hole for Sam. If the inevitable is going to happen, it doesn't need to involve any more torture.

My intuition was correct, and Kiera was out cold when Vincent went to check on her. After a much-heated debate, I manage to persuade him to put an air hole in on Sam's wall. There's no telling when Kiera's going to be in any state to talk, and as much as he threatens them with suffocation, I don't think he wants that to happen. The main thing is that Kiera believes her brother is suffocating when she comes to.

With four pairs of hands helping to pack at one time, the house is down to the bare minimum by night-time. I had expected to do some heavy lifting but apparently all furniture stays in the house, then when they're ready to move, Vincent and Pop disintegrate the house back into the earth. This way it leaves no trace of their existence here.

We're all mentally and physically exhausted, and with an early start tomorrow, we have dinner and go our separate ways. Tyler is still on shift, so Lily takes Tyler's bed, and Vincent and I retreat to his room.

We act as if we've been sleeping in the same bed for years. There's no awkwardness or shyness. As we lie down together, he wraps his arms around me, drawing me closer to him.

"I'm sorry if it came across today that I didn't trust you. Of course I trust you, I just don't want you anywhere near XET."

My stomach ties in knots at the guilt. He shouldn't trust me. But soon enough XET will be my whole life. "Once I'm trained, I want to join you at Headquarters."

His body goes rigid. "If you're so certain you want to be a

part of this life, then Sam and Kiera are your responsibility in the morning."

He's testing me. I don't believe he would make me go ahead with killing them, but at the same time he is expecting me to say no right now.

"Okay." I struggle to control the shakiness in my voice. What if he's serious?

He groans. "You're not a killer. You're my gentle, kind and sweet Kaylee." He nudges his head into my neck and plants a kiss on my shoulder.

Does he have so little faith in my ability to defend myself? To defend the people I care about? I roll over to look at him. "I want to join you in Headquarters."

"You're not ready yet, so why don't we talk about this later?"

Everyone keeps telling me that, as if I'm going to wake up one day and change my mind. Perhaps tomorrow will be that moment after they deal with Sam and Kiera?

I huff as I roll back over and he nuzzles back into my neck, inhaling deeply.

His breathing slowly grows louder and longer, and eventually his arms slacken around me.

CHAPTER TWENTY-TWO

Sleep doesn't come. I eventually wriggle my way out of Vincent's arms and toss and turn for at least two hours.

A small creak in the floorboards alerts me to movement in the hallway. Vincent lies undisturbed beside me and I slowly get out of bed, trying not to wake him. I open the door as slowly as possible, just wide enough for me to get out and look down the hall, but I can't see anything in the darkness. I wonder if I should check on Lily or Tyler, but I figure the sound was my imagination or one of them changing shifts.

I head to the kitchen for a glass of water, but I stop when I notice movement on the front porch. A large dark outline moves under the light of the full moon, heading down the stairs and away from the cabin. I quietly move closer to the front door, my heart thumping in my chest as I recognize who it is.

As quickly and quietly as possible, I follow Pop.

I'm halfway across the clearing at the front of the house before I get close enough. He must have heard my footsteps as he quickly turns around.

"What are you doing?" I talk in a hurried whisper.

"Go back to sleep, child," he replies in a gentle tone. "I just needed some fresh air."

He's fully dressed, including hiking boots.

"I'm not going back inside without you."

"Listen to me," he says sternly. "XET are coming, and if I don't get to them before they arrive, then I don't know what could happen to the rest of you. I won't have that on my conscience."

A lump forms in my throat. "What do you mean they're coming? What's going on?"

"The two kids have internal trackers so it's only a matter of time before XET arrive, that is if they aren't already watching and waiting. There's only one road into this place so I'm going to go and meet them. If I don't put up a fight, then I've been guaranteed you will all be left alone."

"You can't seriously believe that? They're not just going to come here for you and leave Sam and Kiera with us." This doesn't make sense. He said that Sam and Kiera were working independently of XET. "Please, just come back inside and we can talk about this tomorrow."

"They're willing to sacrifice the two kids in exchange for me. Just know that I trust with every ounce of my being that what they're offering can be trusted. I wouldn't be doing this if I weren't absolutely certain of your safety."

There's no way anyone would leave children here to die.

This is all my fault. I need to persuade him to come back inside.

"Pop..." My voice catches as I attempt to plead with him. "You can't."

"There isn't the time, child. Let me do this. Let me play my piece."

I'm distracted by movement out the corner of my eye at

the edge of the clearing. I gasp as four figures move out from the tree line, hands in front of them holding onto items that glisten in the moonlight. Guns.

Pop turns his back to the figures, pulling me in front of him to shield me from them. "*Go*! They will leave quietly with me."

A loud bang echoes through the clearing, and as I look up, Pop's face is covered with dread. I turn around to Vincent and Tyler standing on the balcony. Tyler has his arm around Sam's neck and Vincent is pointing the gun to the sky.

"No!" Pop whispers in horror as they slowly walk toward the stairs.

"Sam?" a female voice calls out across the clearing.

"Mom?" he calls back.

Two of the figures break off from the others and start heading around the edge of the clearing toward the cabin.

Wait. Sam's mom?

Pop turns to face XET and raises his hands in surrender. He takes a step toward them and my body automatically follows his.

"Stop!" Vincent shouts after us.

"Go, child!" Pop demands of me furiously. "Go back to Vincent and let me leave."

Vincent pulls the revolver back. It's so quiet that the sound of the gun cocking echoes through the clearing. Vincent takes aim at Sam.

By now the two figures are almost level with us at the edge of the clearing, and it won't take long before they're between Vincent and us. Vincent, Tyler, and Sam slowly make their way down the stairs.

"God dammit son!" Pop moans in frustration, looking up toward Vincent.

Pop takes another step toward the two figures at the back

of the clearing and the earth vibrates. I look over to Vincent who has an arm pointed to us, and a large wall erupts between XET and Pop and me. Pop pulls me into his chest and then pins us to the ground. I scream as the sound of the bullets penetrates the still air and thud as they land in the earth barrier.

"Cease fire!" The shouts comes from one of the figures who had moved around the side of the clearing.

Tyler lets out an agonizing scream, clutching his face, and Sam has escaped his grasp, heading straight for Vincent.

Vincent's earth wall crumbles as his focus is drawn to Sam who jumps toward him to grab the gun and they fall down the steps together.

My heart skips a beat. "*Nooo*!" I scramble to my feet, ignoring the fact I'm now exposed to XET.

"Kaylee," Pop calls as he chases me.

Sam and Vincent reach the bottom of the steps and time stands still as they grapple each other for control over the gun.

The sound of a gun firing fills the still night, triggering XET to release their bullets again. Pop throws his arms around me and tackles me to the ground.

I crane my neck and watch Tyler tackling Sam. Vincent's body lies unmoving at the bottom of the stairs.

My throat burns as a soul-shattering scream leaves my body and I thrash against Pop as he presses his palms into the floor and a wall of earth encases us like a cylinder, attempting to shield us from the bullets.

The female voice screams out for cease fire again as I scramble to the wall, throwing my bodyweight against it. I take a couple of steps back to load up a wind ball and I trip over Pop, who's kneeling on the ground, panting.

I groan in frustration. We don't have time for Pop to be

getting exhausted. I kneel in front of him and hold my hand out to him to share. It's a risky move given his history of stealing but right now we need him able to defend.

He takes my hand and encases it with his large hands, a warm stickiness to them. I wait for my energy to drain, but if anything, I'm feeling even more fulfilled.

Pop closes his eyes and an overwhelming flood of gray-blue energy enters my body.

"What are you doing?" I look at him with eyes wide and try to snatch my hand away. He holds onto me firmly and lets out a wet cough. Even in the darkness I can see the staining of the fluid around his mouth.

"Pop?" I ask with a shriek.

He doesn't respond, just continues to filter his energy through to me.

"Stop," I beg him, trying to get to my feet to shake him off. He grabs me firmer and pulls me into him, wrapping his heavy arms around me in a bear hug. The stickiness returns, but this time on my cheek at his chest. I move my hand to the wetness, and then look at my fingertips that glisten from the dark liquid. My stomach tenses as I cry out, "No, no, no," and run my hands across his torso, trying to find the cause. He winces as my hand finds the bullet entry wound and I firmly press my hands against it, unable to do anything else as his large arms continue to hold me tight.

"Please stop," I plead again, his gray-blue energy continuing to flow into me but now at a much slower pace.

He looks down at me, attempting to speak but no words come out. His eyes glisten as he gives me one of his large, warm smiles and lets out a sigh. I struggle to hold his weight as his body slumps against me, his eyes emptying and our connection ceasing.

My vision blurs as the tears cascade down my cheeks.

The full weight of his body presses against me and I fight with all my strength to keep him upright; any attempt to deny what's happened. But the weight becomes too much, and he starts falling to the side. With a dull thud he lands on the ground and I stay frozen, staring at his motionless body. My breath hitches as a sob escapes. I look at my shaking hands, stained dark like the night sky.

"No, no, no," I repeat again, grabbing onto Pop's shoulders and shaking him. This can't be real.

As if echoing Pop's fallen life-force, the earth shield surrounding us begins to crumble in a mirror image of my shattering heart.

A shout on the outside of the barrier distracts me and my heart aches as I turn away from Pop. Right now, I have no choice but to refocus. I allow the anguish that courses through my body to fuel me as I rise to my feet with determination, readying myself for what lies outside the barrier. The air hangs heavy around me and I'm tempted to reach out and grab hold of it, but a deeper, more primal sensation calls out to me from below.

With tears streaming down my face I scream out into the night, calling to that deep force below my feet, and the earth rumbles in return. The power stirs within me as the earth wall around me shakes. I grab hold of that power and press my hands down to the ground with all the force in my body, and this time the wall shatters as a dark expanse opens across the field, separating me from the two figures standing at the end of the field. I raise my hands and mounds of earth protrude from the crevice, up into the sky. There's no way they're getting to us anytime soon.

I quickly turn back around to assess where everyone else is and my heart stops in my throat.

Vincent remains motionless on the ground, and one of the figures has his knee on his back. I quickly conclude that they would only be concerned about him moving if he were still breathing. I let out a small breath in relief.

Meanwhile, Tyler is sitting beside Vincent with his hands on his head in surrender. Sam is standing behind him with the gun aimed at him.

The other figure stands unmoving, her aim pointed at me, and I have mere seconds to decide what to do. Unlike last night, I can't risk attacking without having to consider the safety of other people I care about. By the time it would take me to move my arm and attack they'd easily discharge the gun at any one of us. What good are these powers if we can't even defend ourselves against guns?

A wail echoes through the clearing and I quickly turn to the source. There's a silhouette on the balcony. Kiera comes into view, but someone stands behind her. Lily!

Kiera lets out another shriek that fills the empty night as her legs buckle, but Lily continues holding firmly to her wrists.

Kiera sobs, begging for her to stop.

"Wait!" The woman who had her gun pointed to me raises her gun above her head.

"Mom?" Kiera sobs out to the voice. "Mom, please make it stop."

No one else moves. The tension is heavy in the air.

"We just want the grandfather." The woman's voice is firm, but I notice a slight waver.

All attention returns to me and their eyes move to Pop's body on the ground beside me.

The clearing illuminates with a red hue as a bloodcurdling scream erupts from Kiera. The cabin is engulfed in flames and Kiera writhes against Lily's hold, which only makes her scream harder. It causes a flashback of the time I went to grab Lily and ended up with a burned palm. My body tenses as the thought of Kiera's arms underneath Lily's hand.

"*Stop*!" This time it's my own voice shouting out at Lily. This must stop! How do I make it stop? One life is enough tonight.

Kiera's shrieks slow to a whimper and the woman who had been calling out pauses, staring at me as if contemplating. She looks at Pop, then to Vincent and back to her daughter.

"Take Vincent," she commands firmly to the person kneeling on him.

"*No*!" I scream again, racing toward him, halting as the woman points her gun at me again.

The person on Vincent sits him up which causes him to stir. Vincent thrashes about as he comes to and the woman goes to help control him, securing his hands in front of him.

With all the determination in my body I reach out to the air around me, readying to fight. At the same time a ring of fire surrounds us all as Kiera's screams recommence.

"Mom," Sam pleads with his mother as he looks upon his tortured sister.

The woman pauses briefly as she looks around at the situation and then directs her gun at her daughter and my stomach drops. What sort of mother is she? Is Vincent's life really worth more than her daughter's?

I pause.

Maybe that's the key?

I thought my only two options were to let them take Vincent, or fight and risk all of us being killed. But if I can make them believe that they can't take Vincent alive...? This option only risks my life, but my life is nothing without him!

My mouth is dry as I look over to him. This could be our last moment together. My eyes sting as the tears re-emerge. *I'm sorry.*

I swallow the lump in my throat as I reach my hand out. Vincent and Tyler grab at their throats and Kiera's shrieks stop too as Lily falls to her knees, mouth wide. Vincent might be my main target, but I need Lily and Tyler not to interrupt. Plus, if something goes wrong and they can't put up a fight, perhaps XET might leave without harming them.

Sam's mother quickly assesses what's happening. With a look of desperation on her face she points her gun at me shouting, "*Stop!*"

Vincent reaches his hands toward me, staring at me with love. He nods and my insides shatter. Is he trying to say he's happy to die rather than be captured?

My heart threatens to stop beating as the earth in front of me rumbles and a barrier emerges, cutting him from view. I press my hand against the barrier, fighting back the tears but never releasing my hold on the three of them.

The fire diminishes and when I look to my left, Lily's motionless body lies on the balcony. Sam is already grabbing Kiera. He pauses as he looks at me with the gun by his side. He has a direct line of sight, but he turns to his sister and picks her up in his arms, her forearms raw.

Vincent's shield begins to crumble in front of me. He mustn't be far off passing out.

If XET don't fall for my plan, what then? Do I let them take Vincent? Try to fight them all myself? Or continue to withhold oxygen until he dies? Another tear escapes at the thought. Will his shield hold up long enough after he passes out? I can only hope that their retaliation on me is quick.

"Enough!" the woman's voice shouts out desperately.

My heart flutters with hope but then I hesitate. This could be a trick.

"We'll go!" she shrieks again, pleading.

With racing heart, I crouch and peer around the edge of the barrier. There's no way I am looking out at normal level in case she has her aim ready.

As she comes into view, she's standing with both hands raised in surrender.

"Leave now or I'll kill him," I order.

Tyler's lying on the ground unmoving with Vincent beside him spasming as he succumbs to the lack of oxygen. I slowly reduce my grasp on Tyler and Lily seeing they've both fainted–any longer and I might cause permanent damage–but I continue with Vincent. I can't let them think I'm wavering in my resolve.

The woman looks down at Vincent and orders everyone to retreat quickly.

I almost let out a sob as they run from view. It worked! As soon as they're far enough away, I release my hold on Vincent who inhales with a gasp, rasping as he continues to breathe deeply. He stumbles to his feet, coughing, and attempts to run on unsteady legs toward where XET left. He shoots ball after ball of debris in their wake, but they're gone. He falls to his knees.

A deafening silence falls over the clearing.

I look over at the wide gaping hole that runs across the plateau with large bulbous mounds of earth protruding out. What happened to the two people on the other side?

Vincent turns around and scrambles for Tyler, feeling for a pulse and looking up at me with wide eyes. I'm not sure if he knew I wasn't trying to kill any of them.

"He's fine," I reassure him.

As if proving the point, Tyler's eyes open and Vincent slowly helps him sit up.

Vincent looks to me and begins smiling, but then his eyes widen at the blood staining my body. He hurries to me, running his hands over me for the cause, pleading for me to say I'm okay. But I can't speak.

He doesn't know yet.

A lump forms in my throat as I turn my gaze out to the distance and Vincent follows them to the lifeless body shining under the moonlight.

"Pop?" Vincent's voice is laced with pain which makes my heart ache.

He takes a step toward Pop, but I grab hold of his arm.

"We can't be certain that XET have left." Each word is filled with regret but I'm not willing to risk his safety.

A movement to my side catches me by surprise as Lily joins us. She too looks at Pop's body, all emotion drained from her face. She steps forward and raises her arms, a ring of fire emerging around the entire edge of the field. She pushes her arms forward and the fire stretches itself back, heading out into the forest. If XET are still here, they won't be for much longer.

I hold her arm and share everything I have left. Her fire rises into the night sky as it grows in strength. Vincent grabs on, followed closely by Tyler. Together we pool our energy into Lily and the fire roars with life. With us all connected, combining our energy, I shiver at the sheer magnitude of strength I sense coursing through us. The fire stretches out, leaving a darkened earth in its wake.

We hold onto each other, shaking with despair as the fire slowly fades and Lily releases her hold on it. If XET are game enough to attack again, they'll have to wait until the scorching earth cools enough to get through.

Lily and I stay back as Vincent and Tyler sprint for Pop. They fall to their knees beside his body, embracing each other as they grieve for their grandfather. Time stands still as their heartache echoes through the field. I reach out for Lily's hand and we stand together, being a comforting presence for one another.

Vincent is first to stand up. He places a hand on Tyler's shoulder and uses the other to maneuver the earth out from under Pop, which lowers him down into the ground. Once he's fully covered, a plant begins to sprout. Its branches twine and leaves spurt as it grows to shoulder height.

Vincent and Tyler both make their way toward us but despite the glaze in his eyes, Vincent is all action.

He shouts orders to grab anything left inside and to meet back at the pickup.

I want to reach out and hold him, but right now that's not what he needs. I do what he asks and head inside to grab the few items left.

My hands shake as I pack my bag. The adrenaline from tonight lingers.

Within two minutes we're back in front of the cabin. Vincent pauses briefly and lets out a sigh as he looks up at the cabin then raises his hands. The building shakes as it slowly begins to disintegrate into the ground, as if sinking in quicksand. Sweat beads at his forehead, and Tyler places his hand on Vincent's shoulder, helping provide energy as the last of the cabin sinks from view.

We quickly climb into Vincent's pickup with Tyler and Vincent in the front. Vincent creates a bridge over the gaping crevice that allows us to get back to the dirt road and Tyler runs water over the still scalding earth as we drive through the fire damaged area.

Vincent doesn't look at me the whole trip, despite me

being clearly visible in the rearview mirror. Does he know that this is all my fault? If I hadn't let Pop down with Sam and Kiera, then he wouldn't have tried to leave. But then XET might have attacked while we were all still sleeping. He needs to know the truth, but not now.

We arrive home and wake a very groggy Aunt Amy. I'm already halfway up the stairs when she emerges at the top, worry written across her face as she grabs at her nightgown. Lily charges into her arms and Aunt Amy holds on tight.

"What's happened?" She searches my face for answers, gasping at the blood.

"They found us, Aunt Amy. We need to go!" It's amazing how such a short response can have so much impact.

"Go get dressed and gather your essentials. Five minutes!" She speaks to the two of us firmly, yet in a soothing manner.

I grab some clothes from my room and run to the bathroom to get changed. I remove my clothes but when I look down my body is painted red. I turn my hands over, making fists, and my skin aches as the blood cracks and flakes, having dried on the car ride home. A sob escapes as I flash back to the moment my hands found the entry wound. There was nothing I could do.

I jump in the shower, desperate to get clean. The water runs red as the blood washes away. I grab a sponge and rub my skin until it aches as I eliminate any traces of tonight. I don't have enough time to dry properly so the clothes cling to my body as I head back to my room and pack a backpack worth of essential items.

By the time I come back outside, they're all waiting in the pickup for me, with Vincent behind the wheel.

Right now, we need safety, and the safest place we know is Headquarters. We figure XET might be expecting that course of action though, so we drive away from the closest airports and head for Hartsfield-Tylerson Atlanta International Airport in the state over.

Tyler has collected all our SIM cards and thrown them out the window. We can't take any chances of XET knowing our location.

I lean against the door frame.

It was only yesterday that I was so certain about my future. Train. Join Headquarters. Destroy XET. But in twenty-four hours I've shown that I don't have what it takes. And worst of all, I still need to confide in Vincent that I allowed Pop to talk to them alone. Will he ever forgive me? He only just declared he loved me. I wonder if he'll still feel the same.

Pop truly was trying to prevent this whole fight from happening. And it seems as though Sam was being true to his word about protecting the rest of us in exchange for Pop. They were hesitant to fire, and only changed tactics once they saw Pop had died. But why was Vincent the replacement? His life obviously holds a lot of value in their eyes, especially when you consider the price they were willing to pay for Vincent.

And once we're at Headquarters, where do we go from there?

So much uncertainty lies ahead, but as I look around at some of the most important people in my life, I'm grateful that I'm not alone. I need to dig deeper inside myself to become stronger and more resilient.

Focused.

Determined.

Tonight, I may have let people escape who could end up taking the life of someone in this very car. XET are already responsible for the death of someone I loved dearly. It stirs a deep rage within me. I will never forgive myself if another person is hurt because of me.

I look out into the night to keep guard. I regenerate so that I can take immediate action should the need arise and as the energy builds within me I welcome the additional strength of the gray-blue energy that has fused with my gold.

INDEX

ACKNOWLEDGMENT

Firstly, a massive thank you to my husband, two young children, mum, dad, and sister. For putting up with me while I tried to juggle everything in my life, especially in the months prior to the release of PAIRED where I lived and breathed this book. For the endless calls and messages. For when I already knew the answer but continued to give you multiple options, then became frustrated when you chose differently. You are probably sighing with relief that the book is finished, but this is just the beginning. Love you all!

To my many friends, old and new, for your assistance in critiquing. In particular, my writers group *The Saturday Chapter*. This story would not be where it is without all your help.

To my editor, Sally Odgers, for your invaluable assessment and editing services. To JS Cover Designs for your brilliant book cover. And to The Nutty Formatter for putting together the final pieces to bring my dream to reality. It has been a pleasure to work with you all.

And finally, to all my readers. I cannot explain the happiness that I experience when someone chooses to read my writing. I love to create stories outside of real-world possibilities, and I hope I was able to take you on an enjoyable journey with PAIRED.

Keep updated on the latest news at:
KRISTENTEMPLE.COM

Instagram: @kristentemple_author_artist
Facebook: Kristen Temple - Author and Artist
Twitter: @ktempleauthor

THE BILLIONAIRE'S COWGIRL

BILLIONAIRE HEARTS SERIES BOOK THREE

EDITH MACKENZIE

The Billionaire's Cowgirl (Billionaire Hearts Ranch Book #3):

Images © DepositPhotos – valuavitaly, lake & underworld 1.

Cover Design © Designed with Grace

❀ Created with Vellum

Sometimes the hardest thing to do is to leave behind what you thought was true, for the real truth